George's latest idea is brilliant — why not raise funds for new schoolbooks — and at the same time raise enough for a new 'aerodynamic' skateboard for George! His friends Stick, Tub and Kev are not impressed because they know that George's ideas usually spell trouble, but they end up agreeing to help anyway.

Then Sharon Taylor, who looks like a shampoo advert and makes George swoon, offers to help with the fund raising, and Stick's awful little sister Julia takes charge of publicity. Things start to go wrong very quickly. Packing groceries for donations leads to headline news: NEAR RIOT AT LOCAL SUPERMARKET. Chaos reigns when the wave machine goes out of control at the sponsored snorkel. And to cap it all, the gang are chased by two strange men who seem extraordinarily interested in Kev's garden gnome . . .

What do we do now, George?

by
Helen Magee

PIP
POLLINGER IN PRINT

Pollinger Limited
9 Staple Inn
Holborn
LONDON
WC1V 7QH

www.pollingerltd.com

First published by Macmillan Children's Books 1989
This large print edition published by Pollinger in
Print 2007

A CIP catalogue record is available from the
British Library

ISBN 978-1-905665-67-9

For Stephen and Matthew

Chapter One

George looked at the skateboard. It was the most beautiful thing he had ever seen — apart from Sharon Taylor. And it didn't look at him as if he had just crawled out from under a stone the way Sharon Taylor did. It just sat there in the shop window begging to be bought. It wasn't the old fashioned kind either, so thin that your feet hung over the edge. It was broad and curved at the front with a tail at the back and smooth running wheels. It had tiny little fins just above the back trucks. Aerodynamic, thought George. Perfect.

His birthday was three months past and Christmas was not for another six months yet. He hadn't a snowball's chance of getting it. He ran a hand through the sandy hair that always flopped over his forehead no matter what he did to it.

"Great, isn't it?" said a voice behind him.

Well, behind him and up about five inches. Paul Graham, also known as Stick, had put in a lot of growing since he had turned thirteen, mostly in the legs. He reminded you of a stick insect and walked with a sort of bounce, as if he hadn't got used to his height yet.

"Hi, Stick," said George.

They had been friends since infant school. Four of them had gone around together. George, Stick, Tub Robson and Kev Chisholm. Not that Kev had ever been infant sized. Kev's Mum said he walked early because they didn't make buggies big enough for him.

"They're running a competition for one of those," said Stick looking at the skateboard.

"Competitions are a mug's game," said George. "They're always fixed beforehand. How much does it cost to enter?"

"It's free," said Stick. "All you have to do is think up a name for it."

"You mean like Styler or Transmission?" said George.

"Suppose so," Stick shrugged. "Anyway, I've entered. I mean it's free. Why not?"

"Advertizing stunt," said George. "You'll never win." But he pushed open the door of the shop anyway, just to get a better look at the skateboard. The entry forms were lying in a pile on top of the counter.

"What name did you think up?"

"Asteroid Two," said Stick. "Good, eh?"

George looked at him.

"Why Two?"

He shrugged.

"I don't know. It just sounded good."

George was filling in his name and address on an entry form, just to pass the time. Well, it was free, wasn't it?

"We'll have to get a move on or we'll be late," said Stick. "What have you got first period?"

George looked at the bit on the form that said 'write your suggestion here'.

"Classical Background."

"Boring," said Stick. "I tell you, last week it was all about some horse that could fly — I hadn't a clue what old Burns was talking about."

"Lives in a world of his own," said George. "Latin and stuff. I mean hardly anybody in the school does it. Dead languages — what's the point? I mean, how many ancient Romans are you going to meet in the High Street?"

"I've got Economics — double period," said Stick. "So hurry up. Turnbull's grim if you're late."

George scribbled down the first thing that came into his head and shoved the form through the hole in a box on the counter.

"Economics is the thing," he said following Stick out of the shop. "Learning how to get rich quick."

"Huh," said Stick. "If it's so easy how come Turnbull's teaching us and not living it up in some tax haven enjoying his millions?"

"You need flair," said George. "Turnbull's got no imagination, no ideas."

"Some people get too many ideas," said Stick, "naming no names, of course."

George ignored that.

"You need ideas," he said. "You have to take chances, risks. You have to look at the market and see where the gap is."

"Oh yeah, like selling homework answers to the first years and getting them wrong?" said Stick.

George took a swipe at him with his school bag.

"That was French," he said. "I never said I was any good at French."

"And what about the toffee apples? It cost you more than you made to get that stuff to clean your mum's cooker."

"OK so I haven't hit on the right scheme yet," said George dreamily. "But when I do . . . when I do . . . ."

"Pigs will fly," said Stick as they turned in at the school gates, "or you'll meet an ancient Roman in the High Street."

George was always dreaming up schemes to get rich quick. Ever since Stick had known him, George had been full of daft notions. Even in infant school. It was his hobby, like some people made model aeroplanes. They all had some kind of mania, Stick thought. Take Tub Robson. With him it was food. And Kev — his was wildlife and conservation and things. Last year it had been saving the whale and a few months ago it was the big old oak trees they were going to cut down to make room for the new supermarket car park. The trouble with Kev was he went over the top at times. Anyway, he chained himself to one of the trees and threw the key of the padlock away. Eventually the fire brigade had to cut him loose. Still, he made his point. It got in the local paper and the Friends of the Earth or somebody got involved and the trees were saved. The car park had to be moved to another site and Kev got a social worker. He was furious at the time — kept asking why he had to have a social worker — till he met her. She was interested in plants and that kind of stuff and was helping him to plant a wild garden. Knowing Kev, wild was about right. But then his dad had given his mum this garden gnome and now she wanted to build a patio over Kev's wild garden. His mum didn't call it a wild garden though — she called it a patch of weeds. Poor Kev. That gnome was trouble and Kev really hated it.

As for Stick himself, he had enough on his plate keeping out of his sister Julia's way. And then there was that dog his mum had bought. He couldn't make up his mind which was worse — Julia or the dog. Probably the dog. At least his dad wasn't always going on at him to take Julia for a walk. Or maybe his dad was worst of all. Dads were a terrible hassle. That's where George was lucky. He hadn't ever had a dad. Maybe that was why he was so bossy — being just him and his mum. He reckoned George must get away with murder. His mum never seemed to get on to him even when he did daft things. Usually she just laughed and said he would grow up soon enough. And that made George wild. His schemes never came to anything and they were mostly harmless — mostly. The thing was not to get involved. He was a good enough guy, George, except for his mad ideas and Sharon Taylor. Sharon Taylor, thought Stick. She was the most stuck-up, bossy girl in their year but George couldn't see it. There was no accounting for taste. Maybe it was because she was the only person George knew that ordered him about. Usually George did the ordering. Even so, it was pretty hard to take — seeing George jump when she snapped her fingers. This thing he had about Sharon Taylor was worse than his get-rich-quick schemes.

Stick sighed. As far as he was concerned, George could get rich on his own. Getting rich was too risky. He turned to say so and shook his head. George was in a world of his own, dreaming up more schemes. There were times when you could talk to him and he wouldn't even hear you. Then he would come out with the latest plan and it was always worse than the last one. The safest place to be when George was working out a foolproof plan for getting rich was anywhere else.

"See you," said Stick.

George didn't hear him. In fact Classical Background came and went without George really noticing. So did morning break. Wheels had begun to turn. He really wanted that skateboard.

Chapter Two

Half-way through French George realized he was on the wrong page of the book. Not that it made much difference. French was a mystery to him. Ask any first year.

Mr Martin, the French teacher, asked him a question.

"Sorry, Mr Martin. I've lost the page," he said.

The teacher's face took on its resigned expression, the kind George was used to seeing on his mum's face. Like last week when he tried setting up a business weeding gardens — with her Hoover. He had seen this advert on TV for some machine that sucked up weeds and grass. He still couldn't understand why you couldn't just use an ordinary Hoover, except that it hadn't worked. He wondered if his mum would get a new one. He wondered if they could afford a new one.

"Find the page," Mr Martin was saying patiently.

George dived head first into the sports bag at his feet.

Mr Martin spoke again, louder this time, "George. What are you doing?"

"Looking for the page, sir," he said.

Mr Martin was quite good — for a teacher. He didn't throw chalk or dusters and he wasn't the boring, sarcastic type either, like a lot of them. But even George could see he was really hanging on to his temper — like Tub Robson and the last cream bun in the Universe.

"Are you trying to be funny?" he said.

Just for once, George wasn't.

"No, sir," he said.

"Then find the correct page."

He made another move towards the bag.

"AITKEN," thundered Mr Martin. "I shall lose patience with you soon. Will you find the page in your book."

Light dawned at last on George.

"It's not in the book," he said. "When I said I had lost the page I meant it was missing, not there, lost. I thought it might have fallen out into my bag." He spoke slowly, to make sure the teacher understood. Some of them were really thick. Not Mr Martin though — at least, not usually. He must be having a rough day, thought George.

15

Mr Martin walked slowly towards him. He reached down and picked up George's book. A few pages drifted loose and floated to the floor.

"How long has this book been in this state?" he asked. His voice was quiet.

"Since I got it," said George.

"And was the page there when you got the book?"

George blinked. What a daft question.

"I don't know," he said. "They all look the same to me. I mean, they're in French."

He looked round the rest of the class. They were grinning. None of them were very good at French in this class. Mr Martin's face had gone really pale. He looked as if he was trying to say something but his mouth wasn't co-operating too well. He reached out a hand to George. George noticed that it was quivering slightly, then the bell rang and the class was in uproar as they stampeded for the door. George flung the book into his bag and began to gather up the loose pages. He stuffed them in as well and, when he looked up, Mr Martin was over by the window looking out. George stood there for a moment watching the teacher. He was grinding stubs of chalk to dust on the window ledge.

"Nervous breakdown," said Kev Chisolm in his ear. "Seen all the signs before. My dad went just like that when I dropped the gnome through the roof of the garden shed."

George's interest was immediately caught. "You never told me about that. What did you have against the garden shed?"

Kev punched him casually on the elbow and George winced.

"The garden shed was an accident," he said. "It was the gnome I was trying to smash. I hate that gnome."

He turned to George, emotion showing clearly in his face, which was unusual. Kev usually looked kind of stunned — like a gorilla who had walked into a door.

"I got it all the way up to the roof," he said. "It wasn't easy, you know. Then it slipped the wrong way and fell through the roof. I meant to push it off and smash it on the rockery. Still, it doesn't look too great any more," and he swaggered off down the corridor kicking people lightly as he went.

Don't suppose the garden shed does either, thought George.

It was the latest thing with Kev — this gnome his dad had got for the garden. Kev had got it into his head that if it wasn't for the gnome his mum wouldn't want this patio and he could keep his wild garden. For all he was such a clumsy guy, he was great with plants and things. His solution to the problem was simple — destroy the gnome.

They had all had to listen to him going on about it for weeks now. One thing you could say for Kev, George thought, when he got on to a subject he stuck with it.

Speaking of sticking with a subject, George began to wonder if he could persuade the PE teacher to buy in skateboards as gym equipment. He could imagine the answer he would get if he asked. This school can't even buy books and you're asking for skateboards. Maybe it was thinking that or maybe it was the French book or even having to share a Maths book with Tub but something began to stir deep in George's mind. Tub was crunching fruit drops which drowned out the sound of the teacher's voice and left him with a mind free to ponder. It came to him that his class was sharing an awful lot of very tatty text books these days. He had heard a lot of teachers going on about it recently. But then teachers were always going on about something. It wasn't as if they expected you to take any notice.

It was later, when he was queuing up to use the bunsen burner in Chemistry, that the idea came to him. That was the great thing about ideas. If you left your mind open long enough they just sort of arrived there. Teachers never appreciated that. They were always going on about you not paying attention. Einstein probably had the same problem when he was at school. Kev had him by the lapel at the time, asking him if he thought the Chemistry teacher would suspect anything if he asked her what acid would do to concrete.

"How many bunsen burners do we have in this lab, Kev?" said George.

Kev's brows drew together. "Who wants to know?" he said.

George sighed. Kev wasn't really tough. He just liked to act tough. It was the way he looked. People expected him to be tough.

"Just count them, Kev. I can't see past you."

Kev turned and George lurched slightly as the fist that held his lapel clenched in concentration.

"Eight," he said.

George pondered. Eight, and twenty-four pupils in the class.

"Well, what do you think?" said Kev.

"What about?" said George.

"The gnome and the acid," said Kev.

George looked up at him, "Sounds like a horror movie," he said.

"Eh?" said Kev.

George unclamped the fist from his lapel.

"Look, why don't you convert a bunsen burner into a blow lamp and try that on the gnome?"

He should have known better. A light appeared in Kev's eyes.

"You know, George, I don't care what anybody says about you and your daft ideas. You've got brains." And he shouldered his way casually to the front of the queue.

There wasn't time for George to have a go on one of the bunsen burners and as they left the lab he looked round the benches.

Seven, he said to himself. I thought Kev said eight.

Kev was just going out of the door. There was a length of rubber tubing hanging out of his blazer pocket.

"Keep trying, Kev," shouted George after him. "Eventually that gnome will die of embarrassment."

"You OK?" said Stick behind him.

"I've had an idea," said George.

Stick groaned. He should have known. He'd seen the signs.

"Is that the time?" he said making a break for freedom. But speed wasn't his thing. Height was his thing.

George grabbed him. "The public park tonight. At the fountain. Half past seven. Tell anybody else you see."

"I have to take the dog for a walk."

"Bring the dog," said George.

"I think I might be coming down with Bubonic Plague."

"Fight it," said George. He was used to feeble excuses.

"Julia will want to come," said Stick and held his breath. There was silence. Julia was eleven years old and had been poison ever since they were kids. She tried to tag along no matter what you said to her. You could say anything to her and she still didn't go away. George knew. George had been trying it for years.

"I'll think of something," said George.

"It's no good," said Stick. "She's like a bloodhound. You're wasting your time. She says she's going to be a newspaper reporter."

Julia was a pain in the neck. Julia was always butting in where she wasn't wanted. Julia just kept on and on till you noticed her and most people would do anything, say anything, promise anything to get rid of her. Julia would be a really good newspaper reporter.

George brightened. "That's it," he said. "Publicity. We'll need publicity. Bring Julia."

Stick looked at him, stunned, "Sorry, George. I thought you said 'bring Julia'."

"I did," said George.

Stick looked at him closely,

"Are you all right?"

"Bring Julia," said George.

Stick shook his head.

"I'm in shock," he said. "Nobody's ever said that to me — bring Julia. And now you've said it — twice." He bounced off shaking his head sadly. "It's the end of civilization as we know it. The dog's better company than Julia."

Chapter Three

George arrived first. He was sitting on the low wall that surrounded the ornamental pond throwing stones at the fountain in the middle. It was a favourite thing with him, mainly because of the statue of a horrible simpering cherub which stood on top of the fountain. Every so often a stone would glance off a passing duck but mostly he got the cherub square between the eyes. He noticed a black furry thing bobbing along the top of the hedge on the opposite side of the pond. Sure enough, in a minute, Stick bounced into view. An empty dog lead dangled from one hand.

"Where's Julia?" said George.

"She wouldn't come," said Stick. "She thought it was a trap."

"What kind of trap?"

Stick shrugged and bounced at the same time. It was positively balletic. "I don't know what kind of trap but you can't blame her. I could hardly get the words out. I mean — asking her to come?"

"She must have thought you were acting suspiciously," said George.

"Too right I was," said Stick. "It was weird."

George looked at the dangling lead. "Did the dog think it was a trap as well?" he said.

Stick looked around wildly.

"It was there a minute ago. If I've lost it I'll get killed. Mum only got it last week. It's a pedigree."

"A pedigree what?"

"Dog. What do you think?" said Stick.

Sometimes Stick was as bad as Kev.

"Why don't you just call it?" said George.

"Call it what?"

George had a sudden picture of Mr Martin grinding chalk into dust. No wonder — he had to put up with this kind of thing for a living.

"Its name," said George.

"I can't remember its name," Stick said trying to set off in all directions at once. He always looked as if he had more than his fair share of arms and legs. "It's one of those huge long things."

"What, the dog?" said George.

Stick looked at him.

"No, idiot, the name. The dog's insignificant. Don't you ever listen?"

"I've been listening. It doesn't seem to work," said George. "Look, what do you usually call it?"

"Bozo," said Stick.

"Shout Bozo, then," said George.

"That wouldn't do any good," Stick said. "It doesn't answer to Bozo."

The stone lay, tempting, in George's hand. He laid it down carefully on the wall beside him. He couldn't afford to kill Stick. Not just yet anyway. He might need him.

At that moment a small hairy object shot out of the hedge. Stick sort of collapsed on top of it and clamped the collar round its neck. The dog looked a bit dazed.

Tub was the next to arrive. "I just stopped off at the chip shop on the way down," he said.

"Didn't you get any tea at home?" said Stick. For all he was as thin as a rake he was as interested in food as Tub was.

"Mum's put me on a diet," said Tub.

Stick looked shocked. "That's cruelty to children," he said. "You should do something about that."

"I am doing something," said Tub. "I'm going to the chip shop."

"Social worker," said a voice and they all jumped, even the dog.

Like a lot of big people Kev could move really quietly.

"That's what you need, Tub," he said pummelling Tub's stomach. "They're great. Mine got me more pocket money. Said I needed — what was it now?" His brow furrowed with effort. It was painful to watch. "The chance to explore the limits of my responsibilities. How about that then?"

He was really pleased with himself.

"And have you," said Stick, "got to the limit, I mean?"

"Dad says I have," said Kev looking not at all bothered.

Tub was staring. There was something even odder looking than usual about Kev. It was a minute before George realized his eyebrows were missing.

"Hi, Kev," he said. "What happened to your eyebrows?"

Kev's massive hand shot up to the place where his eyebrows had been.

"Singed off," he said.

"Accident was it?" said Tub rubbing his stomach. You could tell he thought it served Kev right and why stop at the eyebrows.

Kev nodded. "Not that I'm blaming George," he said and George nearly fell into the pond from fright. "It was a great idea making a blow torch but I don't think I got the connection right."

"What connection?" said Stick.

"On the Calor gas bottle," said Kev. "It's been sitting outside all winter and the label had come off."

They were all staring at him.

"Anyway, no harm done," said Kev. "The caravan's not a total write-off and the social worker is there again. She's talking about getting somebody to come and see Dad. Says he needs help."

There was silence. They all stood looking at Kev. Maybe it was the absence of eyebrows. In most people an eyebrow here or there might not be missed but in Kev's case they had added a certain something to his face. Without them he looked like one of those Easter Island statues they had had a film about in Art History. They could hear the rhythmic thud of tennis balls on the courts behind the hedge. George couldn't stand the strain any longer.

"OK, I give in. Where does the caravan fit into the picture?"

Kev grinned.

"The Calor gas bottle was attached to the caravan," he said.

Talking to Kev was like playing a fruit machine. You had to get the combination right.

"Was the caravan still there when you left?" said George.

Kev scratched his head.

"Some of it," he said.

George gave up. He didn't have time for social chitchat. He looked round the little group. Stick and Tub were staring at Kev in a glazed kind of way that might have been admiration. The dog was whimpering as best it could which wasn't much because Tub was standing on its lead and its head was on the ground gasping for air. Stick yanked the lead from under Tub's feet, the dog yelped and the spell was broken.

"Right," said George. "Gather round. Eve had this idea."

Stick groaned, "I thought you might have forgotten about that."

"You don't know what it is yet," said George.

"I'd like to keep it that way," said Stick. "The last time you had an idea I got my pocket money stopped for a month."

"Get a social worker," said Kev. "They're great for pocket money." Kev was always going on about his social worker, trying to make them jealous. Sometimes George wondered if he got into bother on purpose just so that they wouldn't take his social worker away. At any rate he never seemed to mind getting into bother and he got on really well with her.

"Look," said George. "Just listen to it. That can't do any harm."

They didn't look convinced. George had a brainwave.

"Tell you what," he said. "Listen to the idea and if you don't think it's the best yet you can chuck me in the pond."

Tub thought of all George's other ideas. "It wouldn't have to be very good to be the best yet," he said.

Stick was looking almost cheerful. "It's worth the risk," he said. "You promise now? We really can chuck you in the pond?"

"Scout's honour," said George.

"You haven't been a scout since you demagnetized the Kestrel Patrol's compass before they did their orienteering badge," said Tub.

George sighed. Tub was always harping on his past. "They all got their survival skills badge out of it, didn't they?"

"I was in the cubs once," said Kev.

"That's impossible," said Stick. "They don't make the uniforms that big."

"I didn't have a uniform," said Kev. "I was only in it one week."

"What happened?" said Tub.

"They gave me all my badges and said I could leave the cubs and join the scouts when I was old enough."

"What cubs did you go to?" said Tub, interested. The only badge he had ever got was cooking.

"The hut down by the common," said Kev.

"There isn't a hut down by the common," said Stick.

Kev grinned. "There used to be," he said.

Nobody asked what Kev had done to the hut.

George leapt off the wall brushing the dog lightly with his foot. It yowled.

"Now listen you lot. Just shut up and listen," he roared.

Tub looked offended. "You don't have to go mad," he said. "We were only waiting till you were ready."

"I'm ready. I'm ready," yelled George.

He settled once more on the wall. The dog cowered.

"You know how teachers are always going on about not having enough books or equipment — blaming the Government, the education system, us even?"

Nods all round. They all knew the feeling. Half an hour's lecture when you got a book you didn't even want in the first place.

"Well then," said George. "How about starting a scheme to raise money? Think about it. Who could refuse? It's a good cause. What we have to do is think up a few projects. We'll need publicity. We can do all the usual things — sponsored walks and jumble sales and maybe come up with a couple of original ideas as well. We'll make a fortune."

They had a strange expression on their faces. George couldn't quite place it but he thought it might be hate.

"For school books?" said Stick as if he couldn't believe his ears.

"You're right, Stick," said Tub. "It was a lousy idea. What are we waiting for? Let's throw him in the pond."

They advanced on him slowly, silently, menacingly.

"Wait. Wait, I'm not finished," said George.

"That's what you think," said Stick.

He tried to back away — difficult since he was sitting on the edge of the pond. Even the dog was baring its teeth at him. He looked at it, mesmerized, then suddenly it keeled over and lay on its side, dead. Well, well, thought George. I didn't know I had it in me. What a talent.

Someone spoke from the other side of the pond, "Why, George, I think that's a wonderful idea."

They all froze — except for the dog. It wasn't doing a lot anyway.

"Oh, no," said Tub.

"Not her," said Stick.

If Kev had still had his eyebrows they would have been drawn closely together.

George's voice got all gummed up, as if he'd just swallowed a rubber banana.

"Hello, Sharon," he said looking stupid.

She was wearing a tennis skirt and white tee shirt and her long blonde hair stirred gently in the breeze. She looked like a shampoo advert. She smiled at George and he nearly fell in the pond without any help from the rest. It was so unexpected. They had been doing the genetic scale in Biology and George reckoned that Sharon rated him round about toad level. He didn't see the look of hopelessness that passed between Tub and Stick. Kev was looking like King Kong with toothache.

Sharon floated towards him swinging her tennis racquet. "Has anyone seen a tennis ball?" she said. "I'm afraid I misjudged that last shot a little." She giggled and Stick shuddered.

"Oh, there it is," she said pouncing on it. "But what's wrong with your little dog? Is he asleep?"

George preened. "I seem to have killed it," he said. "I must have the power, like in that film about the guy that brings down buildings just by looking at them."

"You're thinking of Kev and scout huts," said Tub.

"No I'm not," said George.

Stick noticed the dog for the first time. After all, he was a long way up and the dog hadn't been saying anything.

"You killed the dog?" he yelled. "What did it ever do to you?"

"It was threatening me," said George, "like the rest of you."

"You stood on it," said Stick. "How would you like to be stood on?"

George thought he was about to find out but Sharon was between them bending over the dog.

"I don't think it's dead," she said, "just stunned. The tennis ball must have hit it."

Stick was pulling wildly at his hair, "What am I going to say when I get home with a concussed dog? It might be in a coma. It might live on and on like that for years. I might have to look after it."

Sharon looked up at him with scorn in her blue eyes. "Oh, don't be ridiculous, Paul," she said. "It's coming round already."

Stick looked relieved, then another thought struck him, "What if it's brain damaged?"

George looked at the dog. It rolled its eyes drunkenly at him.

"How could you tell?" he said. "It wasn't that smart in the first place. I mean it can't have much of an inbuilt early warning system if it lets itself get hit with tennis balls. I thought dogs were supposed to have an instinct for danger."

"If you had any instinct for danger you wouldn't still be sitting there," said Stick. You could tell he didn't know whether to attack George or see if the dog was OK. The dog won. He bent down and hauled it to its feet. It looked round vaguely and lay down again. Stick began talking to it frantically. George ignored him.

"I'll have to go and finish my match," said Sharon, "but I must say I admire you, George. I never thought you had it in you to do something like this."

For the first time George thought he might be getting somewhere with Sharon.

"I didn't really kill the dog," he said. "Remember?"

She shook her head impatiently, "No, no. I mean the project. Come round after school tomorrow. I'll have had some ideas by then."

She smiled at him as she turned away,

"You can listen to me practise my cello."

George was struck dumb. It was too much.

"Right," said Tub as she disappeared round the hedge. "Let's throw him in the pond. Come on, Kev."

George found his voice. He hadn't told them the most important bit yet.

"Percentage," he yelled.

"Eh?" said Kev.

"Percentage," George repeated. "You don't think we're going to do this for nothing, do you? It's the way charities work — percentage for this, percentage for that. If you're good at it you hardly have to give any of it away."

"My mum says that's a scandal," said Tub. "Making money out of good causes."

"Only if you're not the one getting the percentage," said George.

Tub nodded. "I can see that," he said.

Kev seemed to have missed the point. Probably because he was still on fractions.

"Back off, Kev," said Tub as Kev continued to approach George. "Let's hear the rest."

"What about the dog?" said Stick. "He deserves to be thrown in the pond for the dog's sake."

"It was nothing to do with me," said George. "It was the tennis ball."

Stick looked puzzled. "It feels as if it's your fault," he said.

"Everything always feels as if it's my fault," said George.

A voice spoke,

"I want my cut."

They all looked around.

"Did you hear that?" said George.

"It came from the hedge," said Tub. They looked at the hedge. It was a tall, loose kind of hedge. Good for pushing people into.

A figure began to emerge slowly. It looked a bit like a matchstick with mange. Bits of hedge stuck up from its short curly hair. It was Julia.

"I want my cut," she said again. "And if you don't let me in on it I'll tell Sharon Taylor what you're really up to."

George pondered. She really would be good at publicity and she really would go running to Sharon.

"OK," he said making his voice sound grudging. It wasn't that hard when you were talking to Julia. "You're in — so long as you don't tell Sharon."

She looked a bit thrown by that, as if it had been too easy. Then she smiled,

"Called your bluff, didn't I?"

"Eh?" said George.

"You thought if you asked me to come I would stay away."

George sighed. Julia was as straight as a corkscrew. He threw a last stone at the cherub and thought it rocked a bit on its pedestal.

"I'll need to take the dog home," said Stick. "I don't think it's well."

Quite a lot of people stared at them as they trooped out of the park. They were an odd looking bunch — Kev minus his eyebrows and Julia with bits of hedge sticking out of her hair like camouflage. But it was definitely the dog that got the old-lady-out-for-a-walk sympathy vote as it wavered uncertainly at the end of its lead. All in all it hadn't been the dog's day.

As they passed through the park gates Julia said, "There was a fire engine at your house when I came by, Kev."

Nobody mentioned the caravan.

George, for one, was busy. He was trying to work out how much they would have to make to get a percentage big enough (divided by five) to pay for the skateboard. Whichever way he looked at it, the sum seemed to be the wrong way round.

"Have you done your homework?" said his mum when he got in.

"Oh, Mum," said George. "What's the point?"

"The point is, you won't get any qualifications if you don't pass your exams."

The way George looked at it, he would do better to leave and get a job and then his mum wouldn't have to work so hard. She said she enjoyed it, meeting people in the shop but she got tired sometimes being on her feet all day, especially when she did overtime.

He went to do his homework, just to keep her happy. Time enough to fight the battle when he was old enough to leave school. That was the only thing about his mum — wanting him to stay on at school. Apart from that she was OK — for a mum.

Chapter Four

Next day George hung about after French. Mr Martin was collecting books. It didn't take long. There weren't that many of them. He seemed to be a bit more normal today. He was piling the books into a low cupboard as George came up behind him.

"Mr Martin?"

"Ugh!" The teacher raised his head too quickly, banging it on the cupboard door.

"Oh, Aitken," he said. "What are you doing here? The bell's gone."

"I just wanted to ask you something," said George. Mr Martin straightened up kicking the door shut.

"The answer's no," he said, "but I suppose you want to ask anyway."

George ignored that. He'd heard it so often.

"You know this school has got hardly any books," he said. "And the ones it has got are a mess. And look at the equipment — bunsen burners and things. Calculators for instance," he added thinking of the sum he couldn't do. "It's a disgrace."

"Good Lord," said Mr Martin. "And there was I thinking you only popped in to pass the time between acts of vandalism."

"Oh, come on, sir," said George. "You know I'm not a vandal."

Mr Martin rubbed his head, "OK George. It must have been the bump on the head. Still, you must admit, you're not in the school choir."

"What's that got to do with anything?" said George.

"It is indicative of a certain sort of attitude," said Mr Martin.

"Eh?" said George.

"Forget it. What did you want to ask me?"

George put the idea to him as clearly as he could. He didn't mention the percentage angle.

"Well, what do you think? Will we get permission?" he said when he had finished.

Mr Martin rubbed his head again.

"Did you bang your head as well?" he asked.

George tried to look offended.

"What's the angle?" said Mr Martin.

"Angle?" said George. "There's no angle. It's our future that's at stake, you know. It might be tough on you having no books to teach with but it's worse for us. You're dealing here with a generation that's going to grow up uneducated."

"I know," said Mr Martin. "Believe me, I know. And you think books are going to make a difference?"

"Well that's the idea, isn't it?" said George. "That's what you're all going on about all the time."

Mr Martin locked the cupboard.

"OK. OK. I'll get the Headmaster to see you after morning break. Be there, but I still want to know what the angle is."

Morning break wasn't too pleasant for George.

"Why did you have to go and tell him?" said Stick.

George explained patiently, "Because, dope, we'll need permission. You can't just go collecting money for something without permission. It's the way charities work. People get suspicious otherwise."

"Martin's suspicious already," said Tub.

"Only normally suspicious," said George. "Only the way teachers always are. It's part of their training. He doesn't know . . ."

"Know what?" said Sharon as George broke off.

"Nothing," he said. "I just meant he doesn't know us well enough to realize how concerned we are."

She looked doubtful. "I know you well enough," she said, "and I'm surprised. Not suspicious exactly, but surprised." George looked at her. Even school uniform looked OK on Sharon.

"I've changed," he said. "I'm a better person now."

"Crawler," hissed Julia and kicked him on the ankle.

Kev came out of a dream, "Sharon, you're brainy. What does percentage mean?"

Everybody began talking at once and Stick dug Kev in the ribs. Stick had sharp elbows. It was lucky Sharon never took any notice of Kev.

"Tell you what, George. I'll come with you to see the Headmaster. I'll have to go to History first and explain of course," she said.

"Oh, sure. Thanks, Sharon," said George.

She smiled at him. That made three times.

It was a strange feeling to be standing outside the Headmaster's door knowing you hadn't done anything wrong — yet. He knocked and went in. Mr Martin was already there. He seemed to be talking to the Head about the school trip to France.

"I've just been explaining your idea, George," he said as George shut the door behind him.

The Headmaster looked at George across his desk. He was pretty normal for a Headmaster. Careworn, a bit ragged round the edges. He looked as if he expected to be hit in the eye with a custard pie any minute.

"Aitken," he said. "I don't quite understand your wanting to do this. You're not in the school choir, are you?"

George sighed. There was a knock on the door and Sharon drifted through in shades of blonde.

"Excuse me, Mr Redfeather," she said. "I promised George I would come and help him explain."

The Headmaster relaxed.

"Oh, you're involved in this are you, Sharon?"

Sharon was in the school choir.

From then on it was a breeze. Banda machine, school hall — it was theirs for the asking. The only fly in the ointment was that the Head had put Mr Martin in overall charge. Not that Mr Martin had volunteered. In fact when George remembered what Mr Martin had been saying when he came in, he was certain that some kind of deal had been done. He was sure he had heard mention of

Mr Martin not having to take the school trip to France if he took this on.

Funny way to take your percentage thought George. Shocking how every man had his price.

Once outside the Headmaster's room Sharon thanked Mr Martin prettily and said she must be getting along to History now. Mr Martin leaned on the wall, hands in pockets. He looked kind of dogeared.

"That's what tipped the balance," he said nodding in Sharon's direction as she disappeared round the corner.

"I can't sing," said George before he could mention the school choir again.

"Not the point," said Mr Martin.

He unfolded himself and began to walk along the corridor with George,

"Not in a hurry to get back to your class?"

"It's only English. I can speak English," said George.

"See what I mean. It's the attitude, George, the attitude."

"What's wrong with wanting to raise money for the school?" George said.

"Nothing at all," said Mr Martin. "It's just that I can't help feeling that I'm missing something."

"What kind of thing?" said George.

"The angle," said Mr Martin. "It's just not like you."

"Maybe I've changed," said George.

Mr Martin stopped and looked at him.

"It's a possibility," he said. "Must be the love of a good woman."

George blushed. Mr Martin laughed not unkindly. "Bring me your plan of attack by Friday lunchtime," he said, "and I'll go over it with you."

All through English George fumed. Talk about blackening a person's character. It was enough to make him do the thing for real just to show them. Forget about the percentage. He caught himself up, sickened. See what they had driven him to? He mustn't let ideas like that take hold of him.

"Are you all right, Aitken," said Mr Bell the English teacher. "You seem to be muttering to yourself."

"Sorry, sir," said George. "I don't think I'm quite myself."

Mr Bell smiled pleasantly.

"Well, don't think we're not grateful for that," he said. Mr Bell was the sarcastic type.

They all met by the fountain again that evening. George arrived without Sharon. He knew it had been a great honour to hear her practise her cello but his ears were sore. Maybe she hadn't played it for a while. She had seemed a bit upset when she let him in. All he'd said was there was a terrible noise coming from her front room and did she have a cat. What bothered him now, apart from the buzzing in his ears, was how to tell the rest what she had — no they had — no she had decided.

Stick was there already — dogless. That was a plus. Julia was with him which kind of cancelled out the dog.

"No walkies tonight?" said George.

"It won't come out," said Stick morosely. "It's got agoraphobia."

"That's not what Mum said when she saw the lump on its head," said Julia.

Stick winced as if the memory was painful. "She took it to the vet," he said. "It's got a black eye."

"Oh, give it a rest, Stick," said George. "It's a black dog. Who's going to notice?"

"Where's Sharon?" said Julia. "I thought you were going to help her practise her cello. Did she stand you up?"

George gave her a look. "She's still practising her cello," he said. "I left to come and meet you lot."

"She threw you out," said Julia.

"She did not throw me out. We agreed I should go." You had to be firm with Julia. Give her an inch and she took a mile.

"She threw you out," said Julia again.

"Only because I didn't recognize the tune she was playing," said George.

Stick wavered for a moment. He still couldn't get it into his head that George wasn't responsible for the state of the dog. The habit of a lifetime was too strong. He came down on George's side.

"That's lousy. I mean if you've never heard a tune before how can you recognize it?"

Julia was not the type to give up. "What was the tune?" she said.

"The National Anthem," said George.

Tub and Kev arrived together. George was glad to see that Kev hadn't lost any more bits of his anatomy. He decided to plunge straight into business and ignore Julia who was singing God Save the Queen.

"We've got to get a list of activities to show Martin on Friday," he said. "Any suggestions?"

"We could have a sponsored walk," said Stick.

"Boring," said Julia. At least it stopped her singing.

"I don't like walking," said Tub. "Why is she singing the National Anthem?"

"Nobody's asking you to like it," said George.

"Like it?" said Tub. "It sounds like a cat with the heebie jeebies."

George didn't want to hear about cats. He also had the feeling he was losing his grip on this meeting.

"Forget Julia. She's stopped now anyway. I meant nobody's asking you to like walking. Just think of the percentage."

Tub and Kev spoke together.

Tub said, "Forget Julia — some hope."

Kev said, "What's a percentage?"

Julia barged Tub and squared up to Kev, all in one fluid movement. Her eyes were about level with the logo on his sweatshirt.

"Look, Kev," she said prodding him. "The percentage is what we get out of it. Think of it as a fee, the rake off, our cut."

Kev brightened up. "I don't mind walking," he said.

Tub looked unconvinced.

"OK," said Stick, "what do you like doing?"

"Snorkelling," said Tub.

George weighed up the odds. He was going to need all the help he could get if he wanted to put Sharon's idea across after that business with the National Anthem. "OK, we'll have a sponsored snorkel. It's different. What else?"

"A jumble sale," said Julia.

"Now look who's being boring," said George.

"It might be boring," said Julia, "but it's profitable. It's a well known fact that you make more money out of jumble sales than any other kind of fund raising."

"Says who?" said Stick.

"Says Mum," said Julia. "AND she says she's got a lot of junk she wants to get rid of."

Stick thought of the trouble he was in over the dog. If his mum wanted a jumble sale . . .

"Sounds a good idea," he said.

"Chicken," said Tub.

"You didn't hear what she said about the dog," he said.

"OK," said George. "That's a sponsored snorkel and a jumble sale."

"Besides," said Julia, "we might find something valuable. People are always finding things worth thousands of pounds at jumble sales."

Tub chimed in, "Right enough, my mum always watches the *Antiques Roadshow* and just about everything comes out of attics and jumble sales and things."

Tub's mum watched the funniest programmes.

"Anything else?" said George.

"We could do packing at the supermarket," said Kev. "It's always crawling with scouts and things doing that." They all looked at him. Nobody had expected Kev to have an idea.

"Great," said George before anybody else had recovered. Now was the moment while they were still in shock from Kev making a suggestion. "Sharon had an idea," he said moving casually to the other side of the pond. He aimed a stone or two at the cherub for luck. Better to put as much distance between himself and the rest as possible. He might have to fight his way out. "She thinks we should have a concert."

It took a moment for this to penetrate, then they all spoke at once.

"I'm not going anywhere near a stage," said Tub.

"You mean singing and dancing and that? No fear," said Stick.

"Mum will make me do my rotten ballet," said Julia.

Surprisingly Kev wasn't that bothered.

"I could play the drums," he said.

"I didn't know you played the drums," said Tub.

"I don't but I could."

"What do you mean, you could?" said Stick.

Kev looked puzzled. "It's easy," he said. "You just hit them. I'm good at hitting things."

"A concert then," said George quickly. "And we don't have to worry about organizing it. Sharon's going to do that. I'll make a list of the suggestions and give it to Martin on Friday."

It hadn't been as bad as he had thought, thanks to Kev. He felt quite kindly towards Kev.

"How's the gnome?" he said.

"It got a bit chipped when the back of the caravan blew off," said Kev.

"Well, that's progress," said George.

"Oh, it's not much," said Kev modestly. "It gave me an idea though."

"What, another one? You want to watch that, Kev," said Tub.

"Shut up, Tub," said Stick. He found himself strangely drawn to the saga of the battle between Kev and the gnome.

"I thought I would try a pickaxe," said Kev.

"Have you got a pickaxe?" said Julia impressed.

"No, but I know where I can get one."

"Handy, that," said George. "I suppose it'll be practice for the drums."

His mind was on other things. Like working out how to fix the percentage. With Mr Martin in charge it wouldn't be easy. And then there was Sharon. It had all seemed so simple when he first thought of it. Then he thought about the skateboard. It was worth it.

Chapter Five

One good thing about the project was that they were all let off afternoon classes on Friday to prepare the publicity material. Mr Martin had approved the list and given them a list in return. It was a lot longer than theirs had been. They all gathered in the resource centre after lunch.

"I never thought there would be this much to do," said Tub.

"We have to be properly organized," said Sharon. "Now, Philip, you can get started on the posters while I do the stencils for the banda machine."

They all looked round — even Mr Martin. Nobody had come in.

"Who's Philip?" said George.

Sharon looked meaningfully at Tub. He was still looking round to see who had come in. He stopped.

"Oh, sorry. It's me. I forgot."

"I didn't know you were called Philip," said Julia.

"I'm not," said Tub. "I'm called Tub. I've always been called Tub but Philip's my name."

"Why don't you call him Tub. Everybody else does. Even the teachers," said Stick to Sharon.

Mr Martin nodded in agreement.

"Nicknames are demeaning," said Sharon. "Don't you think so, Mr Martin."

"What's demeaning?" said Kev.

"Nicknames, cloth ears," said Tub.

"Well, Sharon, sometimes they can be a sign of friendship," said Mr Martin.

"No, I mean what's the meaning of demeaning?" said Kev.

"I can't work out the question," said Stick.

"Look, Kev," said Mr Martin, "if I called you Godzilla, that would be demeaning."

"People call me that all the time," said Kev.

George smiled. It was nice to see someone else on the receiving end for a change. He tried to think of something really demeaning to call Kev. It was impossible. He looked at Mr Martin's list instead.

"Posters, leaflets, concert tickets, collecting can labels, sponsor sheet forms," he said. "We'll be here all night."

"Not if you let Sharon organize you," said Mr Martin. "I'll be in the office if you need me."

"Trust a teacher to avoid all the work," said Julia when he'd gone.

"You can work the Banda machine, Julia," said Sharon. "I've finished the design for the leaflet. You run it off while I get on with the sponsor sheets."

"Thanks a million," said Julia.

After several false starts she managed to get the sheet in the right way round and right way up. There seemed to be a good deal of purple ink all over her.

"Why don't we have a photocopier like normal schools?" she said.

"We do," said Sharon, "but the Banda's cheaper. Now, George, you make a start on the concert tickets. Paul, you can help George."

"What can I do?" said Kev.

"Good question," said Tub.

Sharon looked doubtful.

"I suppose you could take over the Banda machine and let Julia get started on the labels for the collecting cans."

"Good," said Julia. "My arm's sore already."

Kev took over willingly. Nobody complained when sheets started to fly out of the machine like bullets. He had to do something.

By the time they had finished, Julia had managed to smear the purple ink from her face into her hair. Kev's arm was hanging limply by his side. Tub's knees were sore from crawling around the floor doing posters and Stick had nearly sliced off three of George's fingers with the guillotine while he was helping him cut up the tickets. Sharon looked terrific as usual.

Mr Martin poked his head round the door. He was looking nervous.

"Mr Hughes is outside," he said. "He wants to lock up."

Mr Hughes was the janitor.

"Just finished," said George. "We'd better get out. Everybody take a bundle of stuff." Everybody did. Opinions differed about who ran the school, Mr Redfeather or Mr Hughes, but most people would have come down on the side of the janitor. He stood outside as they passed him, jangling his keys and counting them as they came out. He was always counting them. Nobody knew why.

"Kids," he said to Mr Martin. "Nothing but trouble."

Mr Martin smiled, "Anybody would think the school was run for their benefit," he said.

The janitor nodded and began locking up. The group trundled off down the corridor.

"Wasted on him," said George to Mr Martin sympathetically.

"How do you know I wasn't serious?" said Mr Martin.

George grinned. He liked Mr Martin. It was a pity they couldn't let him in for a cut of the profits but that would be going too far. Besides, he was getting out of having to take the school trip.

"I've phoned the supermarket manager," said Mr Martin "He has agreed to let you pack tomorrow morning. I've also got some juniors lined up to lend a hand."

"Juniors?" said George. "We don't want juniors."

"Take what you can get, George," said Mr Martin. "They were the only ones I could force into it."

Chapter Six

Looking back on it, packing shopping at the supermarket was a breeze compared to the rest of the week. None of them thought so at the time. After all, when you read things in the paper like NEAR RIOT AT LOCAL SUPERMARKET you don't rate it as a success. Nevertheless they were to look back on the supermarket fiasco as an oasis of calm, a practice for the real disasters. George met Stick on the way there. They walked across the car park together. George was thinking about the skateboard — as usual. There was a long sloping ramp up to the main doors of the supermarket. George was imagining himself skimming down it on the skateboard. It would be brilliant.

"My mum says she's coming to do her shopping here this morning and she wants it packed free," said Stick.

George shook his head, "I hope you told her that was corruption."

Stick gave him a look. "You must be joking."

They walked up the ramp towards the store, past rows and rows of shopping trolleys. George looked at them in awe.

"Are we going to have to pack all those?"

Half a dozen juniors had turned up looking depressingly eager. Sharon handed out sticky labels which she referred to as their official collectors' badges. She stationed them all at a checkout each. She also said she would be acting in a supervisory capacity.

Tub snorted, "That means she won't be doing any work. Why can't she just say so instead of showing off how many big words she knows?"

"What's the charge?" said a junior called Amanda.

"There's no charge," said Sharon. "People will make a donation."

"Some hope," said Julia.

"And you must not rattle the collecting can under their noses," said Sharon. "I'm putting them at the end of the cash desks so that people will be free to make whatever contribution they want."

"How are we going to make money that way?" said Stick. "Why don't we just charge them fifty pence each?"

"It's a charity, Paul," said Sharon. "You've got to allow them to give what they can. After all you can't charge an old age pensioner the same as everybody else."

The junior called Amanda looked at Stick as if he'd just mugged her granny.

"Now if anyone wants their shopping wheeled out to the car park you have to catch my attention," said Sharon. "I'll get one of you who isn't too busy to do it. We have to finish at twelve. OK. Any questions?"

"Only what did your last slave die of," said Julia under her breath.

The rest didn't say a thing. There was no point with Sharon in an efficient mood. Stick began to wonder what had ever made him think George was bossy.

Business was a bit slow to start but once it built up George began to see a problem. By the time he had finished the packing, the shopper had paid the cashier and dropped some money in the can. Nobody but nobody handed him their money. He looked round at the others. It seemed to be the same with them. So, if the money all went straight into the cans, how was the percentage to be made? He didn't have a customer so he allowed his mind to turn the problem over. He looked round the store. Outside the big glass walls he could see several people with collecting cans. It seemed to be some kind of flag day. Inside he counted two lottery stalls, a kitchen competition and several slot machines. Talk about a pay-as-you-enter supermarket. Shopping seemed to be a minor activity as far as he could see. Everybody's at it, he thought. Then the solution hit him. All he had to do was hide one of the cans at the end. Simple. Well, simple so long as Sharon was out of the way. He might have to create a diversion.

It was an hour or so before George noticed a steady trickle of people coming back to complain. Several of them were demanding in loud voices to see the manager and a small group of angry looking women had gathered round Kev's checkout.

"Look," said one. "See what he's doing. No wonder my eggs got broken."

"Biscuits right at the bottom with all the tins piled on top," said another. "It's a disgrace. If they can't do it properly they shouldn't be allowed to do it at all."

"I want the money I put in that can back," said another, "and a new packet of cornflakes."

The woman Kev was packing for was surrounded by the knot of women. Kev was carrying on regardless. George had a look at his technique. It was simple but effective.

He just turfed the stuff into a carton as it came off the conveyor belt and if it wouldn't fit he hammered it down till it did. It didn't do the shopping a lot of good but at least it got everything in. Sharon appeared just as the manager arrived looking like thunder. George couldn't hear what she was saying to him but the melting look was having its effect. He was getting visibly calmer.

With a strength he would not have thought her capable of she reached out a hand and yanked Kev away from the groceries he was reducing to pulp. It must be her bowing arm, thought George. He hadn't realized playing the cello developed the muscles.

"George," she said as she passed dragging Kev behind her, "I'm putting Kev outside." She made him sound like the dustbin which was probably the way she thought of him anyway. "If there are any trolleys to be wheeled to the car park he'll do it," she went on.

"OK, Sharon," said George. "Anything you say." He only just stopped himself saluting.

Things got gradually quieter as the trail of Kev's customers finally dried up. By that time the manager was handing out free groceries to anybody who as much as said good morning. At quarter to twelve George decided it was time for action on the percentage front. Sharon was patrolling the checkouts like a prison guard and the assistants were keeping a wary eye on the packers. The only one that was not being watched was Kev. George would have preferred one of the others but there was nothing else for it.

Kev had just wheeled a loaded trolley out on to the ramp beyond the glass wall. George waited until Sharon's back was turned and began to wave to catch his attention. Kev waved back and grinned. George ground his teeth. If he was quick Sharon would never notice he had gone. He nipped across to the window.

"Create a diversion," he mouthed to Kev.

"What?" bellowed Kev.

George waved his hands. "Shut up," he mouthed. His breath was steaming up the window on the inside. Kev tried to wipe it clear on the outside and looked puzzled when nothing happened. George moved a little and put both hands round his mouth, "Create a diversion," he mouthed again against the glass.

Kev put both hands up to his own mouth. "What?" he yelled.

George saw it coming. For a moment he stood rooted to the spot staring at Kev's trolley. It could have been happening in slow motion. George lunged forward to stop it and banged his nose on the glass. It began to bleed. He didn't notice. He was watching in

61

silent fascination as the trolley that Kev had been holding on to before he put both hands to his mouth set off slowly down the ramp. Kev was banging on the glass trying to attract his attention. The supermarket had not been open long so the trolleys were still in good condition, none of this rusty wheel jamming rubbish. By half-way down the ramp it was picking up speed nicely and making straight for a row of empty trolleys.

If it had been deliberate it wouldn't have happened. It fitted itself neatly into the first empty trolley. There was a moment's pause before the long, long line began to move. Kev's trolley had been heavily loaded and it was no time at all before it picked up speed again adding a few more trolleys on the way. All in all there must have been about twenty of them all neatly fitted together. They made a low rumbling noise as they gathered speed down the ramp. By this time other people were beginning to realize that there was some kind of free entertainment going on outside. Gradually the window filled up with silent watchers, the cash registers stopped buzzing, the flag sellers fell silent. Even the slot machines grew quiet as the crowd craned to see what was happening. The snake-like line of trolleys travelled on towards the bottom of the ramp going at a fast lick now and glinting prettily in the sunshine. It was heading straight for one of the concrete bollards that divided the car park from the supermarket forecourt.

There was a crash as the front trolley came in contact with it and the line split asunder like a shining cluster of asteroids. After that it was the noise that really took the attention. Car brakes squealing, horns hooting, the crunch of metal on metal. George could have stayed and watched but he remembered something more important. He slipped smartly back out of the crowd and hid the collecting can from the nearest cash desk under an upturned carton. He had the feeling they would not be staying long. For the first time he noticed he was covered in blood. He was puzzled for a moment before his nose began to hurt. After it was all over certain pictures stayed in George's memory — like the store manager standing there pale and trembling saying "They should never have built that car park at the bottom of a slope. I can't understand what they were thinking of."

"The trees," said Kev.

"What?" said the manager.

"Nothing," said George. "Ignore him."

The manager rounded on him, "I don't know how, but this is your fault and if you ever set foot in this store again I'll have the police on you."

And, worse than that, the junior called Amanda saying, "Oh look what I've found under this carton. It must have fallen over," and handing the collecting can he had hidden — their percentage — to Sharon.

Sharon didn't say a word on the way home and nobody complained when she stalked on ahead.

As it happened, Kev was the first to speak, "What were you saying to me through the window, George?"

"Create a diversion," said George.

"What's a diversion?" said Kev.

Nobody answered.

When George got home his mum said, "What happened to your nose?"

"I walked into a plate glass window," said George.

"Dreaming again, George," she said as she hauled him off to the bathroom. "One of these days you'll walk into real trouble."

Chapter Seven

Nobody was really surprised when Mr Martin met them coming out of assembly on Monday morning and told them the Headmaster wanted to see them. They filed in silently and stood in front of his desk. They jostled a bit, each of them trying to get to the back. It had to stop when they finally wedged themselves back against the door in a clump. There were only the six of them — George, Stick, Sharon, Julia, Kev and Tub. The juniors had not been made to come which George supposed was fair enough. He didn't mind that but he would have liked to see the junior called Amanda get it in the neck.

The Head looked at them sadly. He was looking as if somebody had hit him in the eye with that custard pie at last. He did a quick double-take when he saw Kev. George didn't blame him. Kev's eyebrows had started sprouting again, not everywhere, just the odd tuft here and there.

"The supermarket manager has been in touch with me," said Mr Redfeather. "He didn't have a great deal of time to spare since he was busy getting ready to leave."

"Where's he going?" said Tub brightening up a bit.

"He tells me he is being transferred to Wick," said the Headmaster.

"Where's Wick?" said Stick.

"He was asking me that too," said the Headmaster. "It's in the north of Scotland, the very north of Scotland. However, he did have time to give me a brief outline of the events of Saturday morning and, although he cannot be certain of what actually happened, he is convinced that you were at the root of it."

They all tried to take a step back which was impossible since they were as far back as they could go. The Headmaster ignored the attempt.

"Can any of you give me an explanation?" Silence.

He sighed and pushed a newspaper across the desk at them. "Perhaps you would like to take a look at this," he said. "It's headed 'Near Riot At Local Supermarket'. Just under the article on the museum theft."

They clustered round as George picked up the paper.

"There can't have been that many cars damaged," said Julia. "The papers are always exaggerating. Just wait till I see that reporter again."

A horrible suspicion flowered in George's mind. "What do you mean 'again'?" he said. "You mean you got in touch with the papers?"

"Well you said I was in charge of publicity," said Julia, "how did I know there was going to be a riot?"

"Good publicity," said George. "You're the one that wants to be a reporter. This is what's called getting a bad press."

"He doesn't say it was anything to do with us," said Julia. "He just says at the end that we were collecting for a school book fund."

The Headmaster interrupted,

"I'm afraid for once I have to agree with Aitken," he said. "He doesn't actually say you were involved but tacking it on to the end of the story like that does produce a certain impression. It's the inference, Julia."

Sharon took over, "I'm afraid we are rather confused ourselves over what happened, Mr Redfeather. Philip, Paul, Julia and I were all busy at the time repacking some boxes that had been brought back."

She shot a look at Kev. If looks could kill he would have been dead and buried. Kev didn't notice.

"Philip? Who's Philip?" the Headmaster said.

"Me," said Tub.

"Oh yes, so it is," said the Head then he looked at George. "And you, George. Do you have anything to say?"

George scented trouble. Calling the boys by their first names was always a bad sign with the Headmaster.

"It did seem a bit daft to have the trolleys all lined up on the ramp like that," he said trying to sidestep the question. "I mean the slightest thing could have done it."

"Yeah," said Kev helpfully, "I mean I only took my hands off the . . ."

George kicked him hard but fortunately the Head never took any notice of Kev — not since Kev fell through his study window while practising abseiling from the school roof. That was a couple of years ago, before he got interested in plants and things, when he still thought he wanted to go into the army when he left school.

"Yes, yes," said the Head. "It seems they are going to change that now but I understand the company will have to pay out a good deal of money in compensation. I would like to think you had nothing to do with it, George."

George would like him to think that too.

"I was behind a plate glass window when it happened, sir," he said.

He could see the Head trying to decide whether to go on with it or let it go. Discretion won.

"All right," he said, "I will accept your word but if there's any more trouble connected with this project, any at all, I will insist on its being dropped, books or no books. You may go."

They didn't need telling twice.

"Not bad, George," said Tub.

"Why did you kick me?" said Kev.

"I have never been called up in front of the Headmaster like that before," said Sharon.

"Where is Wick exactly?" said Stick.

"Do you think he believed us?" said Julia.

"What did you say to that reporter?" said George.

They bickered their way down the corridor and George was in the classroom before he realized he still had the Head's newspaper. He stuffed it in his pocket. He wasn't going back in there if he could help it.

Chapter Eight

Apart from the interview with the Head the week started quietly enough. Mr Martin had been busy arranging events. The sponsored snorkel would be on Friday evening, the jumble sale on Saturday afternoon and the concert on Saturday evening, both in the school hall. George suspected him of trying to get it over with in a lump and said so.

"Nothing of the kind, George," he said. "It suits the janitor to have both on the same day. He's going on a self-defence course the next weekend."

George couldn't tell if he was joking.

Sponsor forms were handed out to all the classes and leaflets telling people not to bring jumble to the hall until after school on Friday. George called a meeting at the fountain for Tuesday evening. They didn't tell Sharon. She was busy organizing the concert and practising her cello. She was playing a solo. George hoped it would be the National Anthem so that he would recognize it this time. With one thing and another he reckoned he had lost a lot of ground with Sharon. Maybe it was the way she had looked at him when she told him that her unblemished record at the school was now broken and she held him personally responsible. He wished she wouldn't talk like that.

"It was Kev that let go of the trolley," George had said. She had given him one of those looks — the kind that made him feel about three years old and backward.

"Am I my brother's keeper?" she said. Sharon was hot on RE.

George didn't say anything. He reckoned keeper was just about right when it came to Kev.

Julia was in a rotten mood.

"I told you," she said. "I knew it would happen. Mum wants me to do my ballet at the lousy concert."

"You think that's bad," said Stick. He wasn't feeling too great anyway because he'd had to bring the dog. It dragged along at the end of its lead choking itself. "Sharon's put me in the choir. She says they need baritones." His voice was a deep growl.

71

"What's a baritone?" said Kev.

"I don't know," said Stick. "She just said they needed baritones and put me in the back row."

"She must mean tall people," said Tub shifting something about inside his mouth. Whatever it was rattled horribly against his teeth.

"What are you eating?" said Julia.

"Fizz bullets," he said. "Want one?"

He held out a paper bag to Julia. She tried to pick one up but they all stuck together in a lump.

"Sorry," said Tub. "I was sitting on a radiator at lunch-time and they were in my pocket."

He broke the lump and offered one of the sweets to Julia. Several scattered on the ground.

"No thanks," said Julia looking at the sticky mess. "I've changed my mind."

"You'll rot your teeth," said George.

"They're not as bad as toffees," said Tub. "Toffees are definitely worse."

"You're the expert," said George. He threw a stone moodily at the cherub and missed. He didn't often miss.

"What's wrong with you?" said Stick.

"What do you think?" said George. His nose was still hurting. "All that work on Friday turning out posters and leaflets. Then getting our heads bitten off by that supermarket guy. Then the Head yesterday. And we haven't even made a penny out of it."

It took a lot to get George down so they did their best, all except Julia.

"That guy's gone to Wick," said Stick, "wherever that is."

"The Head never bothers us if we don't bother him," said Tub.

"We'll make money out of the snorkel," said Kev.

"You're just annoyed because Sharon's gone off you again," said Julia.

George ignored her. He turned to Kev.

"How do we make money out of the snorkel?" he said but Kev was looking at the dog.

"Has your dog got rabies?" he said to Stick.

"No, agoraphobia," said Stick. "You're thinking of hydrophobia."

"No I'm not," said Kev. "I've never heard of hydro . . . whatever it is."

"It's got a black eye," said Julia.

"I thought it was rabies when they foamed at the mouth," said Kev.

Stick looked at the dog and turned pale. Sure enough, pink foam was bubbling out of the sides of its mouth.

"She'll kill me if it's got rabies," he said. "How could it get rabies?"

"It has to be bitten by something mad," said Kev.

They all looked at him. Nobody could actually believe he had bitten the dog. Still . . .

Then Tub spoke, "It's OK," he said. "It's the fizz bullets."

"What, those sweets?" said Stick.

"Yeah, they fizz up when you bite them."

They all looked at the dog. Pink foam was still dribbling out of its mouth and it was hunting about the ground for another sweet. It seemed to have perked up a bit.

"Forget the dog," said George. "How are we going to make money out of the snorkel?"

They all thought.

"We could forge some names on the sponsor sheets," said Tub.

"Then we'd have to fork out more money," said George. "It's less names than you've got sponsoring you we need, not more."

Tub thought for a minute.

"Oh yeah, you're right," he said.

"We could hand in only some of the money," said Stick. "Say people were out when we called to collect it."

"They sign when they pay," said George.

They thought again.

"I've got it," said Julia, "we just forge some extra sheets."

"No good," said George. "The sheets all have to be numbered and stamped with the school stamp. I tell you, it's useless."

"OK, we forget about making money out of the snorkel," said Stick. "There's still the jumble sale and the concert."

"And we do the snorkel for real?" said George.

"Cheer up, George," said Tub. "How about threatening people with a rabid dog unless they give us money?"

At that the dog belched loudly and more pink foam bubbled up through its teeth. It seemed to be grinning.

"Glad somebody's happy anyway," said George. It was hard to let go of the idea of making the percentage on the snorkel.

"Right," he said, "jumble collection every night this week and we'll take the sponsor forms with us. We don't have to be too bothered about getting names but we have to make it look as if we're trying."

"Where are we going to keep the jumble?" said Tub. "Old Hughes won't let it in the school before next Friday."

"We'll just have to keep it at home," said George, "unless anybody has a better idea."

"We could have kept it in our caravan," said Kev, "if we still had a caravan."

"We could have kept it in the hut down by the common," said Stick, "if there was still a hut down by the common."

"No you couldn't," said Kev. He wasn't in the least offended. "That belonged to the cubs. Tell you what though, there's a big old house they're going to demolish round our way. We could find somewhere there to keep it."

"Waste of money," said Tub rattling another fizz bullet round his teeth.

"What is?" said George.

"Employing people to demolish a house round Kev's way," he said. "All they have to do is let him loose in it for a couple of hours."

It was decided that they would keep the stuff in the old house.

"That's fine," said Kev. "I've been meaning to go round there anyway."

"What for?" said Stick.

"A pickaxe," said Kev.

"Ask a stupid question," said Stick.

The gnome was in everyone's thoughts.

"You really hate that gnome, don't you, Kev?" said George.

"If it wasn't for that gnome, Mum wouldn't want a patio," said Kev. "And besides, it's horrible, really horrible. It looks evil."

"It must be bad," said Julia.

The rest nodded. If Kev thought the gnome looked evil it must be really horrible.

"Right then," said Stick, "we'll meet at this house tomorrow then and bring whatever jumble we've got. What time?"

"Eight? Half past?" said Tub.

"Eight," said Stick. "OK, everybody?"

George didn't say anything.

"OK, George?" said Stick.

"I might be a bit late," said George. "I've got to go round to Sharon's at eight to rehearse."

"Rehearse what?"

"Oh, just a thing," said George.

"What kind of thing?" said Stick.

They were all interested by this time.

"A play kind of thing."

They had all the patience in the world. They'd got a scent of something good coming.

"What kind of play thing?" said Tub.

"A Shakespeare thing."

"What, you mean like that thing we did about the fairies and the wall and the guy called Bottom?" said Tub.

"No, something else," said George.

"Hamlet," said Stick. "Alas poor Kciroy, I knew him backwards."

George shook his head.

"What then?"

There was no way they were going to let it go.

"Look, it's nothing," said George. "She just stands on this balcony thing and I talk at her."

"Doesn't sound very exciting," said Tub. "No sword fights?"

"It's Romeo and Juliet," yelled Julia dancing round George. "You're doing the balcony scene with Sharon. What a sop."

George threw another stone at the cherub. It fairly rocked on its pedestal.

"It's all right for you," he shouted. "How do you think I'm going to feel?"

"Oh, Romeo, Romeo," said Julia clutching her tee-shirt.

George stomped off.

"You can't play Romeo with a nose like that," shouted Stick after him.

"She'll make you wear tights," yelled Julia.

George continued to stomp.

"Who's this guy Romeo anyway?" said Kev.

"Romeo?" said Tub. "He's worse than your gnome."

Chapter Nine

Things didn't get much better for George on Wednesday. It was bad enough having to rehearse the balcony thing but Sharon had got him a costume as well. She must have been collecting jumble too. He looked at the things in disgust. There was a dark green velvet waistcoat and a frilly blouse with big sleeves.

"I won't show you my costume. I'm keeping it as a surprise," said Sharon. "All you'll need is a pair of tights and it'll be perfect, George."

"With this stuff, all I need is a gipsy violin," said George then he realized what she'd said. He looked at her in horror. His voice came out in a strangulated gulp, "Tights?"

"Now, George, don't be silly about this. You've got to look the part."

"I'm already going to look like something that's escaped from *The Sound of Music*. I'm not wearing tights," said George. "I'd never live it down."

The thought of Julia rose up before his eyes and he shuddered.

"No tights," he said again.

"You've got to," said Sharon.

George wasn't having any of it. He lost count of the number of times he said "no tights" till Sharon got in a huff and threw him out again.

"We'll see," she said darkly as he slouched off down the path.

George's mind was made up and not even Sharon Taylor was going to change it. She might look like a shampoo advert but he wondered if there wasn't a flaw in her character. There were things you just did not ask a man to do and wearing tights came top of the list. He made his way to the fountain but there was nobody there.

"Tights," he said to the cherub and got it in the eye with a pebble.

He walked on through the bottom gate of the park towards the old house on the far side of the common. On the way he passed the mouldering remains of the cub hut.

"Good work, Kev," he muttered as he passed.

The house looked as if it wouldn't take much to demolish it. Windows were broken and the roof had caved in at a couple of places. Even the DANGER notice had fallen down. He heard the rest before he saw them. They seemed to be arguing. They were in the front hall. The door screeched as he pushed his way through but nobody noticed. They were all talking at once. The hall was so big the sound echoed and bounced around the walls. He stood there for a moment watching them.

Kev was kicking bits of plaster out of the wall with his size nines. Tub was trying to talk through a mouthful of toffee. Stick was perched on the banisters which didn't look too safe with his long legs dangling. He was shouting at Julia. Julia was standing in the middle of them all with an ugly green vase in her hand. She was shouting at everybody. It was anybody's guess who she was thinking of throwing the vase at. Ah well, thought George, they might have their faults but they wouldn't ask him to wear tights.

"What's up?" he said.

Julia turned to him.

"It's these idiots," she said. "They're totally ignorant. I don't know why they bother going to school. It's not as if they've ever learnt anything."

George looked at them.

"So what else is new?" he said. "They've been ignorant for years. They're good at it. If you could get an 'O' level in ignorance they'd be dead certs."

"Have you ever heard of Ming?" she said.

George thought.

"I don't suppose it's the guy that's got the Chinese takeaway on Bellarmine Street," he said.

"Stop trying to be funny," she yelled. "Ming. Ming. Ming."

"Hello, who's there?" said Stick and fell off the banisters laughing.

George made the connection. Art History — Ming Dynasty — priceless porcelain — china from China in fact. Who said education was wasted?

He looked at the vase. It was an ugly looking thing but it looked old. Not that old though — not Ming Dynasty. That was the kind of stuff they kept in museums.

He shook his head.

"It can't be," he said. "Things like that just don't happen. At least, not to us."

"It is," said Julia.

George thought of Tub's Mum and the *Antiques Roadshow*.

"How do you know?" he said.

"Because it says so on the bottom," said Julia. "Look." She turned the vase over and there on the bottom, surrounded by a lot of Chinese symbols, was the word "Ming".

Tub had finished his toffee.

"What's the panic?" he said.

"It's nothing," said Julia sarcastically. "Only that we've got a vase worth hundreds, no thousands, probably hundreds of thousands of pounds."

Stick poked his head through a gap in the stair rails and whistled.

"What, that old thing?"

Kev stopped kicking the wall,

"*How* much?"

"Where did you get it?" said George.

"Here," said Julia.

"Here?" repeated George. "What, just lying about?"

"We were looking for a place to stash the jumble," said Tub, "and Julia found this big cupboard. There was all kinds of rubbish lying around in it. I reckon we won't have to do any more collecting. There's enough for two jumble sales there."

Julia shook her head sadly.

"He still doesn't understand. Look, dope," she said turning on him, "we'll never have to collect anything else in our lives again. We're rich."

"I found the pickaxe," said Kev starting to kick the wall again.

"Why are you wasting time with the boot, then?" said George looking at the hole in the wall.

Julia was dancing round again. The vase slipped and George lunged. He caught it just before it hit the floor.

"Hey, that was good," said Tub. "Why can't you do that when you're in goal?"

"Because the ball isn't worth thousands of pounds," said George through his teeth. "Julia, don't do that again."

"Sorry," said Julia.

That had more effect on them than anything. There was a short silence while it came home to the rest that something serious was going on. It had to be serious. Nobody could ever remember Julia saying sorry before.

"We'll take it to that antique shop in the High Street in the morning," said George.

"They'll ask us where we got it," said Julia.

"Well, we'll tell them," said George. "After all, nobody has lived in this house for years. It's not as if we've pinched it. It was just lying around."

"You don't suppose it *is* nicked," said Tub, "and the thieves have hidden it here."

"You've been reading comics again," said George. "You'll rot your brain as well as your teeth. Would you steal a Ming vase then just leave it lying about in a cupboard? Don't be daft."

"Who did then?" said Stick. "Leave it lying around I mean."

"Some ignoramus who didn't know anything about Ming," said Julia pointedly.

"Who's going to take charge of it?" said George. As if he didn't know.

"You," said Julia. "If I take it home Stick'll probably sit on it."

"We'll need something to wrap it in," said George.

"What's that stuffed down your jacket?" said Kev.

George looked at his Romeo costume,

"Jumble," he said.

"Wrap it in that," said Julia.

George found the Headmaster's newspaper in his pocket and stuffed the vase with it before wrapping it up in the costume. He wedged the whole thing inside his jacket and zipped it up.

"Don't come near me," he said. "I don't want any accidents."

They gave him a wide berth all the way home. George amused himself by hurling insults at them. He would never be safer.

"Nine o'clock outside the antique shop," he said as he turned in at his gate. It was touching the way they had all seen him safely to his door.

"We'll be in trouble for missing school," said Stick.

"It's worth it," said Julia.

George listened to them as they disappeared down the road.

"I forgot to bring the pickaxe," Kev was saying.

His mum was Hoovering the stair carpet when he got in. She didn't have time during the day, what with working and all.

"What's that stuffed down your jacket, George?" she said.

"Jumble," said George.

The Hoover gave a sort of whine and bits of earth burst out of the hose and scattered everywhere. There was a smell of burning rubber.

"You might as well take this for your jumble sale," she said then, when she saw his face, "Don't worry. The weeding was a great idea — the Hoover was on its last legs anyway." She looked tired.

George wanted to tell her that after tomorrow she could have a hundred Hoovers but he thought he would keep it as a surprise.

Chapter Ten

They were at the antique shop sharp at nine. All present and correct. Nobody wanted to miss this.

"OK then," George said. "Let me do the talking. Come on."

They all barged the door at the same time.

"Get back," said George. "You don't want the thing broken at this stage."

They fell in behind him as he pushed open the door. There was an old man behind the counter wearing half-moon glasses. He didn't look very happy to see them.

"Mind how you go there," he said. "There's valuable stuff in here."

He pointed at a notice on the wall. It was one of those revolting rhymes.

Lovely to look at
Delightful to hold
If you should break it
We consider it sold

They stood there nervously. The shop was so crammed full of bits of furniture and china and glass there was hardly room for all of them.

"We've brought you something really special," said George.

"And I've heard that one before," he said sourly. He wasn't exactly a ray of sunshine. "OK let's have a look at it," he went on then, "Careful," as they all crowded round the counter.

George lifted the vase still wrapped in his Romeo costume out of his bag and laid it carefully on the counter. He began to unwrap it.

"It really is special," he said. "Look," and he removed the vase from the folds of the frilly blouse.

The man looked at it and picked it up turning it round. He didn't say anything while he plunged his hand inside and took out the newspaper.

"Where did you get it?" he said at last.

George decided to tell the truth. He couldn't think of anything better offhand.

"Lying about in an old house that's going to be demolished."

"You didn't pinch it?"

"Pinch it?" said George. "No, we didn't pinch it. I told you it was lying about at the back of a cupboard in this old house."

The shop-keeper pursed his lips examining the vase. He turned it upside down and looked at the markings on the bottom. They held their breath.

"All right," he said at last. "I'll believe you though thousands wouldn't."

He had a really original line in patter.

"I'll give you fifteen pounds for it," he said.

They gasped.

"Fifteen," screeched Tub. "Fifteen?"

"OK then, seventeen," he said, "but that's my final offer. I don't say it's not a nice bit of china but this stuff is going out of fashion now. There's a lot of it about."

George couldn't believe his ears,

"Well it would be out of fashion, wouldn't it?" he said. "I mean, it's hundreds of years old — maybe thousands."

"Hundreds of years old?" the old man said. "Don't talk rubbish. It's no more than fifty years old."

"It's Ming," said Julia from somewhere behind Stick. Her furious face appeared under his armpit. "It says so on the bottom."

The old guy nearly smiled.

"So it's Ming, is it? And what do you know about Ming?"

"Not a lot," Tub put in, "only that it's worth thousands of pounds."

The antique dealer leaned across the counter.

"Well, let me tell you a thing or two about Ming. The Ming Dynasty in China was somewhere around five hundred years ago, mainly during the fifteenth century and there wasn't much green porcelain made. Mainly blue and white or maybe some red and a little yellow. And one thing more, they did not write the word 'Ming' in English on the bottom of vases."

His words hung in the air. It took a minute for it to sink in and when it did George wished the floor would open and swallow him up. It was so obvious. It was like the Pyramids having "made in Egypt" stamped across them. How could he have missed it?

"Not Ming?" said Tub.

"Not Ming," said the man.

"Seventeen pounds is quite a lot of money," said Kev.

George thought it was the most sensible thing he had ever heard Kev say.

Julia's face was a picture but she wasn't the type to give up.

"Twenty," she said.

"Seventeen," said the man.

"We'll take it," said Tub.

Stick was counting on his fingers trying to divide seventeen by five.

The shop-keeper reached into a drawer and counted out a bundle of notes.

"Anybody can make a mistake," he said, clearing the newspaper away. He lifted a crumpled sheet and leaned across to them again. "Now something like this is really interesting," he said waving the sheet at them.

George began to feel very uncomfortable. The headline stared out at them, NEAR RIOT . . . but the man was pointing to the story above it.

"That's what you call really old," he was saying with his finger on a fuzzy picture.

They shifted to get a look at it then George froze as he heard the unmistakable sound of something crunching. He hoped it was Tub's fizz bullets. He prayed it was Tub's fizz bullets, but he knew it wasn't. He forced himself to look.

It was impossible to tell what it had been. Now it was just a mass of broken glass under Kev's left foot. The shop-keeper kept calm. You could tell he was keeping calm by the way his knuckles had gone white from gripping the counter. The Art History lesson was over.

91

"Just bring me the ticket," he said, then, "not you," as Kev made a move.

Julia picked up the little white ticket from amongst the fragments of glass and gave it to him.

"Twenty-five pounds," he said and put the seventeen pounds back in the drawer. He pointed to the revolting notice, "You owe me eight pounds," he said.

They couldn't believe it. They had come in here to make thousands and they ended up owing eight. It might as well have been thousands to them for when they counted up they had only one pound forty-three between them.

The man shook his head sadly at them, "It won't do," he said.

He shifted the vase on to a shelf behind him and George thought of making a quick burst for freedom. No use. They would probably end up breaking more things and not getting away. He laid the one pound forty-three on the counter.

"Look," he said gathering up his Romeo costume, "you'll have to trust us to owe you it. We haven't got any more."

The man began to shake his head then he put out a hand and extracted the white frilly blouse from George's bundle.

"Tell you what," he said turning it over, "my wife sells antique clothes. This is a nice bit of lace. I'll take this and we'll call it quits."

George was about to say no way or words to that effect when he became aware of four pairs of eyes on him. He thought of what Sharon would say when he told her he'd lost half his costume. He thought of explaining to the others that it was in fact his costume and not just jumble. The antique dealer was speaking again.

"You can have your one pound forty-three back as well." That did it. If George refused they would tear him limb from limb. There was a quick scramble as the money found its rightful owners. George picked up his share.

"It's a deal," he said.

There wasn't much to say on the way back to school, just the odd comment like,

"It's a mug's game," from Tub,
and

"It nearly cost us money," from Stick.

George, Julia and Kev didn't say anything in case Tub and Stick started blaming them.

They met Mr Martin on their way into school and he gave them detention. They didn't even argue. George was so sunk in gloom that he nearly walked right past Sharon.

"Oh, George," she said brightly, "I meant to say last night but do be very, very careful with the blouse I gave you. I really ought not to have done it because it belonged to my great-grandmother and is something of a family heirloom but I did want you to look nice." George looked at her in horror.

"And, George, you will think again about the tights, won't you?"

She was gone before George could say anything, which was just as well considering.

"Jumble," he muttered to himself. "I thought it was jumble. What's she going to say when she finds out I've sold her family heirloom?"

He thought of telling the others. No point in that — what could they do? He knew what Kev would say — what's an heirloom?

Chapter Eleven

George spent most of Friday avoiding Sharon and trying to work out how to get the blouse back. Mr Martin found him lurking behind a cupboard in his form class during afternoon break.

"You're not supposed to be in here, George," he said.

George tried to look ill which wasn't all that hard.

"I'm not feeling too well," he said.

"Too many late nights?" said Mr Martin. "You should be ashamed of yourself at your age. I hope you're better by tonight. I've arranged with the Sports Centre to get the pool for an hour from seven o'clock. That should give you time to get back here and sort out the jumble for tomorrow."

George shuddered at the word "jumble" but Mr Martin was collecting books and didn't notice.

"Oh, by the way," he said as he picked up the last of them, "Sharon was looking for you. Something about a dress rehearsal for tomorrow night."

This time George didn't even have to try to look ill.

"Thanks," he said weakly, "I'll see her later."

"No, you won't," said Mr Martin, "at least not until tonight. The Headmaster has given her permission to go down to the local radio station this afternoon to give an interview about the fund raising. We should get a good turnout tomorrow."

He cast a look in George's direction,

"You look fine," he said. "Go out and get some fresh air."

"I think I will," said George. "I'm feeling a lot better."

He had been let off the hook — he didn't have to face Sharon till seven.

The first person he met outside was Julia, looking like thunder.

"Have you heard?" she said.

"Oh, God, what now?" said George.

"Sharon and that interview," she went on. "Who arranged it? Who phoned up the radio station? Me. And she goes to the

Head and gets him to send her. What a cheek."

"It doesn't matter who goes," said George. He really didn't mind Sharon not being around at the moment.

Julia looked as if she were about to leap for his throat.

"It was a brilliant idea though," he said quickly. "Terrific."

"You think so?" she said. "Well, I've got an even better one."

"What's that?" said George.

Julia smiled.

"Think I'm going to tell you? You'd just go blabbing to Sharon. Just wait and see." And with that she was gone.

Maybe he should have forced her to tell him what she was up to but he couldn't be bothered. He didn't have long to enjoy himself. Just until seven o'clock. Oddly enough, when seven o'clock came, he had other things on his mind. Stick, Tub and Julia were waiting outside the Sports Centre when he got there. Kev was the last to arrive. It was the sight of him pushing a pram round the corner that drove everything else from George's mind. Kev's left arm seemed to be in plaster. What now, thought George looking at the pram. There wasn't a baby in Kev's family.

"It's the gnome," said Kev before they could ask.

"I thought you hated that gnome," said Tub. "Why are you taking it for a walk?"

"Dad says I've got to get rid of it," said Kev.

"At the Sports Centre?" said Stick. "What are you going to do with it? Enrol it in a karate class?"

A voice spoke from his left elbow.

"It's never too early to start, or too late," said a little old lady. "That's where I'm going. Karate. You're not safe on the streets these days."

She peered short-sightedly into the pram.

"That baby is rigid with cold," she said patting the blanket that covered the gnome. "You'd better get it inside," and she tottered up the steps to the Centre.

Julia looked after her, "Karate? She can barely walk."

George stuck to the point, "Why does he want you to get rid of it?"

Kev scratched his head with his good arm.

"It was after we came back from the hospital," he said. "He put the gnome in this old pram and said he never wanted to see it again so I brought it along. I'll take it round to the school later. It can go in the jumble sale." The others looked at each other. Nobody liked to ask.

"What were you doing at the hospital?" said George.

"Getting this plaster on," said Kev.

They waited. Kev didn't seem to be going to say any more.

The Sports Centre door opened and Sharon appeared.

"Oh, George..." she began. George trembled. Now he was for it. But she caught sight of Kev.

"What happened to your arm, Kevin?"

"Accident," said Kev. "At least, it wasn't my fault. If that old guy hadn't yelled at me I wouldn't have missed the gnome and hit that water pipe. It's only a hairline fracture."

"The arm or the water pipe?" said George.

"Missed the gnome?" said Sharon.

"With the pickaxe," said Kev.

Sharon looked as if she wanted to ask something else but didn't know what. At least it had put George and the dress rehearsal out of her mind for the moment.

Mr Martin appeared round the corner.

"Right, let's go then," he said. "Oh, by the way, Kev, I hope everything's all right at your house. The garden seems to be under a lot of water but I see the fire brigade is there. Glad to see you're looking after the baby. I didn't know you had a new addition to the family." He sprinted up the steps. "Come on, Sharon, we've got to get the time-keepers organized."

They helped Kev up the steps with the pram while he told them about the man that had chased him from the old house when he went to get the pickaxe.

"It was only a rusty old pickaxe," he said. "I thought I had got away then he turns up in the back garden. 'Mindless vandalism' he yells. No wonder I missed the gnome. He gave me the fright of my life."

The next problem was where to put the gnome. They got past the reception desk OK. The old woman was arguing with the man at the desk about the discount for senior citizens. He just waved them on and got back to the old lady. George reckoned she didn't need karate. She could talk anybody to death.

The dressing rooms were empty by the time they got down.

"That's OK then," said George. "We can leave it here. So long as we're finished first we can get back down here and get it out before anybody sees it."

"Why bother?" said Tub. "The man at the desk's not bothered."

"The man at the desk's not the problem," said George. "The Headmaster's the problem.

Do you want to try explaining to him why we've brought a concrete gnome in a pram into the Sports Centre?"

Tub tried to think what he would say to the Headmaster.

"I'm hurrying," he said after a moment and started casting clothes in all directions.

"They'll be started already," said Stick doing the same.

"Not a chance," said George through a mouthful of jersey. "They'll have a speech from the Head about water safety and doing it for the school and all that stuff first."

"Can somebody tie my poly bag on?" said Kev.

Stick was hopping about on one foot getting into his swimming trunks.

"You can't go in the water with your arm in plaster," he said.

"I can if I tie a plastic bag round it," said Kev.

"You're mad," said Tub. "It'll dissolve."

"Look, we haven't time to argue," said George. "Let's have the bag, Kev."

Julia was waiting for them when they got out of their dressing room and they pelted down the corridor to the pool.

"No running," yelled an attendant as they rounded a corner and cannoned into two men coming the other way. They walked on leaving the attendant explaining to the men that only school pupils were allowed in the dressing room area during the sponsored snorkel and heading them off towards the public gallery.

The Head was just finishing his pep talk when they arrived. Surprisingly, the sponsored snorkel had been really popular and the sides of the pool were crammed with kids.

"Four lengths each at most," Mr Martin was saying, "Or else we won't have time to let everybody have a go. Now, who are the first five?"

"Us," said George before anyone else could get in first. Mr Martin looked at Kev.

"Why have you got a plastic bag on your arm, Kev?"

"Protection," said Kev. "In case the plaster gets wet."

"You can't swim with your arm in plaster," said Sharon, "I'll take his place, George."

George looked at her. She had just finished fixing the dividing ropes for the lanes and was still in the water. It was difficult, maybe the hardest thing he had ever done in his life. She was wearing a blue swimsuit that exactly matched her eyes and her hair was kind of floating. She looked like a mermaid.

"No thanks," said George. "Kev'll be OK."

There was no way they could have Sharon free to go down to the dressing room with them — too risky.

"You go with the second lot," he finished.

He couldn't believe it. He had actually turned Sharon down. Her head went up and she looked at him as if he'd just turned into a toad again.

"Very well, but I must see you later about the dress rehearsal. For the sake of the concert, you understand."

George understood only too well.

"Come on, sop," said Julia in his ear.

They did their lengths in record time and Kev got a special cheer when he came out. He'd done the whole thing with the poly bag sticking up in the air. It was amazing. He took the bag off as he came out of the pool and waved the plaster at the spectators. They went wild. Then he looked at his fingers.

"What does it mean when your fingers go blue, I mean really blue?" he said.

Mr Martin looked at them. "It means somebody tied that plastic bag too tight and stopped the blood to your hand."

"Is that bad?" said Kev.

"Depends if you ever want to use it again," said Mr Martin.

"Come on, Kev," said Julia. "We've got to go."

"What about my hand?" said Kev.

"Your hand will be all right," said Stick. "Will you come on."

They got dressed as quickly as they could and wheeled the pram out into the corridor.

"You go and see if there's anybody about," said George to Stick.

He was back a moment later.

"No go," he said. "The Head's in the front hall talking to some people. We can't wheel it past him. He's sure to stop us and ask questions."

"Who's he talking to?" said Julia.

"I don't know. Just people."

"What kind of people?" She seemed really interested.

"Why do you want to know?" said George, suspicious.

"Because I do," said Julia. "I'll be back in a minute." She disappeared round the corner.

"What's she up to?" said George. He had remembered what she had said that morning about having another idea. She was back in a moment, beaming.

"They came," she said.

"Who came?" said George.

"The TV people. I got in touch with them. Said it was great local news and it just so happens they're doing a programme about education cuts. They said they would send somebody along tonight."

"How do you know it's them?" said Tub.

Julia looked at him scornfully, "They're wearing leather jackets and jeans and the Head's being nice to them. They must be TV people."

This seemed to settle it as far as the rest were concerned so George left it at that.

"Look," he said, "we're going to have to find another way out with this gnome."

A voice spoke behind them.

"If you're looking for an easier way out with the pram, I've just passed an emergency exit."

He was a tall man, wearing a suit, so according to Julia's theory he couldn't be a TV person. Maybe he was the director or somebody important. There was another smaller man just behind him. They were smiling. Maybe if they were TV people after all they would understand about concrete gnomes.

"Thanks very much," said George.

The two men led them back down the corridor and round a couple of corners.

"In there," said the taller one. "There's an exit just behind that control panel. Maybe you'd better see if there's room enough to get the pram round."

"Oh, right," said George and they crowded in.

The room was quite small.

"I don't see any exit," Tub was saying when they heard the door click shut. Darkness descended. It was pitch black.

"Who shut the door?" said Stick.

"I can't see a thing," said Julia.

"Where's the light switch?" said George.

They found it at last and switched on the light. Tub was right. There was no exit. Nobody would admit to shutting the door and when they tried it, it wouldn't open. They shook it and rattled it and kicked it in exasperation. Finally Kev hit it with his plaster and winced.

"A lot of good that'll do," said Julia.

George looked at Kev's reddening fingers.

"At least it's brought the blood back to his hand." he said.

"I think it's broken," said Kev.

"Just as well it's in plaster then, isn't it," said Julia. "Look, what I can't understand is why those men haven't opened the door from the outside."

"Maybe they didn't wait around after we came in here," said Stick.

"We were yelling and banging on the door," said George. "They'd have heard that even if they had gone away down the corridor."

"Maybe they locked us in," said Tub.

George gave him a look.

"Too many comics — like I said before."

"What are we going to do?" said Julia.

"Shout till somebody hears us," said Stick. "Somebody's bound to hear us. Right, Tub?"

Tub clamped his lips together then said, "You don't want my opinion. I get them all out of comics. Ask brainbox George."

George didn't seem to be listening.

"George?" said Stick.

"What?"

"We yell, OK?"

"Wait a minute," he said. "I've been trying to picture where we are."

"Locked in a store room," said Tub. "Any idiot can tell you that — even idiots that read comics."

Tub was a bit upset.

"No, I mean if you think of the way we came in," said George, "We must be at the other end of the building from the dressing rooms. There didn't seem to be much at this end but store cupboards. I wouldn't bet on anybody being down this way tonight."

"I'm not staying here all night," said Julia. "Think of something."

"I'm trying," said George. "If you'd all shut up and give me a chance I might be able to."

There was instant silence. Four pairs of eyes fastened on him expectantly. It was worse than the shouting. George couldn't bear to look at them. His eyes ranged round the room, no more than a big cupboard really. They came to rest on the control panel. He moved towards it. Anything was better than looking at the others. It looked a fairly complicated set-up with switches and levers and things. One was for the lighting, another seemed to be something to do with draining the pool and another one was for the wave machine. A plan began to form in George's mind.

"What's the time?" he said.

"Five to eight," said Stick.

"They'll just be finishing in the pool," said George, "We only had it till eight, right?"

"Right," said Stick. "What's the idea?"

"This," said George pointing to a label above one of the levers. "It's worth a try."

They crowded round and he watched their faces as they saw what he meant to do.

"What do you say?" he said.

They looked at each other then Julia said, "Go ahead. Pull it."

George pulled the lever under the label that said *Wave Machine/Master Switch Override*.

They didn't have long to wait after that. The first face they saw when the door opened was Mr Martin's. It was closely followed by an irate attendant.

"I might have known," said Mr Martin.

"Kids," said the attendant pushing the lever back up. "Horsing around. It's a disgrace. You ought to be banned from the Centre, you ought. I'll complain to the school, you see if I don't. Kids. Just wait till I find your headmaster," and he waddled off down the corridor.

"He ought to be a school janitor," said George.

Mr Martin was just standing there looking at him, which was odd because by rights he should have been shouting at them.

"What I can't understand is how you could padlock yourselves in," he said.

George looked at the padlock in his hand.

"No wonder we couldn't get out," he said.

"Who did it?" said Mr Martin.

"I bet it was those two men," said Tub.

George kicked him. He didn't want Mr Martin asking awkward questions about why they had been looking for another way out.

"What men?" said Mr Martin.

"Don't take any notice of him. He reads too many comics," said George. Tub looked as if he was going to blow a fuse but George carried on, "The padlock must have clicked shut when the door closed."

"What were you doing in there anyway?" said Mr Martin. "Have you any idea the chaos you caused? One minute the last group is finishing off, the next they're swamped with waves and all the other kids jump in thinking its a party."

"It was the only way to attract attention," said George. "I reckoned if this was the master switch somebody would have to come down to turn it off. It wasn't our fault we were locked in."

"I'm not so sure of that, George," said Mr Martin, "but I haven't got time to argue with you. I'll have to go and find the Headmaster before that attendant does. Maybe I can smooth things over, maybe not, but in either case I advise you to keep well out of his way tonight."

He snapped the padlock back on the door.

"Activating the wave machine. Why couldn't you just shout like normal people?"

"We tried that," said Stick, "and it didn't work. We just used our initiative."

Mr Martin said something unrepeatable about initiative and George wondered whether getting out of taking the school trip was worth all this trouble to him.

"Sorry, sir," he said.

"So am I, George, so am I," he replied and swept off to deal with the Headmaster.

"Thank goodness that's over," said Stick. "Let's get out of here."

"Wait a minute," said George.

"What?" said Tub, "and if you start talking about me and comics I'll brain you."

"We've lost the gnome," said George.

They all looked round as if they expected the pram to materialize suddenly in front of them.

"What do we do?" said Stick. "We can't go around asking people if they've seen a concrete gnome in a pram."

They had begun to trudge towards the main hall when round the corner came a strange apparition. It was grey haired and elderly and dressed in a karate suit several times too big for it but, more importantly, it was wheeling a pram.

"There you are," said the old lady. "I've been looking for you everywhere. When I saw those men going off with your baby I knew they were up to no good." She seemed out of breath but she chuckled just the same, "Wait till I tell my niece. She says I'm too old for karate. Too old. Why, I hardly got started on them before they ran away. I haven't looked at the baby yet. I hope it's all right. The rug seems to have slipped over its little face."

She reached over to pull back the rug and they moved as one. It couldn't have been better if they had rehearsed it. George got between her and the pram. Kev yanked the pram towards him and turned it round. Stick and Tub moved to either side of it and Julia took the old lady's arm and began to ask her about karate chops.

George was proud of them. What a team.

She was still saying what a good baby it must be and how it hadn't cried at all when they deposited her at the karate class again.

"I just slipped out to go to the Ladies," she said as they left her. "Who would have thought a thing like that would happen? Just wait till I tell my niece."

The Headmaster was in the front hall with Mr Martin so they had to wait till they had gone. They stationed themselves and the pram behind some dismantled trampolines.

"We'll have to get back to the school and sort out the jumble," said Tub.

George was more concerned about getting out of the Sports Centre alive. It was unlucky for him that he peered round the corner just as Sharon crossed the front hall. The Headmaster had gone.

"Oh, George, I'll walk back to school with you and we can discuss the rehearsal," she said.

He heard the sniggering behind him and kicked the nearest leg. Tub yelped.

"The Head's still there," he lied. "Give it another five minutes and I'll see you back at school. My cover's blown anyway."

If there was one thing he would not put up with it was walking back to school with Sharon AND the rest.

"Hi, Sharon," he said breezily, "I was just looking for you."

Chapter Twelve

By the time the others arrived at the school the sorting of the jumble was well in hand. George wasn't feeling too bad either. Sharon hadn't mentioned the blouse and he had arranged to have a dress rehearsal after the jumble sale. They would surely take in quite a bit of money at the jumble and if anybody deserved a percentage of the profits, he reckoned he was the one. A quick trip to the antique shop to buy back the blouse and then round to Sharon's for the rehearsal. And he had handled the question of the tights not too badly either. He hadn't actually said he would wear them but then again, he hadn't said he wouldn't. She had smiled at him when she gave him the tights. The Sharon situation could have been worse. The skateboard situation wasn't so good but there was the concert still to come.

He was standing there looking at a pair of long black tights when the others arrived. He rolled them up quickly and stuffed them in his pocket. No need to give the rest an excuse for getting at him.

Sharon was in an efficient mood and by the time Mr Martin got there they had nearly finished. He drew George aside.

"Talk about luck," he said. "The Headmaster didn't even hear about your incident with the wave machine."

"But that attendant went off to find him," said George. Mr Martin nodded.

"He didn't stand a chance. You know there were TV people there?"

"Julia fixed it up," said George.

"Good for Julia then. They saved your skin."

"How?"

"Look, George," said Mr Martin, "wherever TV people go idiots leap out of the brickwork wanting to be on the box. Well, the word seems to have gone round pretty quickly that they were there and this old woman in a karate suit arrives talking about having rescued a baby from kidnappers. Kidnappers I ask you. Have you ever heard anything more ridiculous?"

George swallowed.

"What happened?"

"They phoned her niece, that's what happened. She came and took her away. Honestly, it's just so irresponsible, letting elderly people do things like karate. She must have got a bump on the head. Jenny says that's the last time she's going. She was against it from the start."

"Jenny?" said George.

Mr Martin coughed. "The niece," he said. "Nice girl. She's a social worker."

George decided not to ask any more. Better to quit while he was ahead and thanks to the old woman he was definitely ahead. If Mr Martin wanted to get mixed up with somebody that had a karate crazed old aged pensioner for an aunt, that was his business.

"What did the TV people say?" he asked.

"They've talked to the Head," said Mr Martin, "and they're going to do some interviews at the concert tomorrow night. They seem quite pleased actually. They were looking for what they called a 'human interest' angle for their programme on education cuts."

George could feel the sweat standing out on his forehead.

"They're not going to film the concert, are they?"

He could just imagine it. Bad enough to have to do this Shakespeare thing but putting it on television. It was too much.

The rest had heard him. They were round like flies.

"Who's filming?"

"Are we going to be on telly?"

"You'll have to wear the tights, George. Make it look really professional."

"You were on the radio. It's my turn to be on TV."

"Quiet, quiet," said Mr Martin. "It'll probably only be a couple of minutes at the end of the programme. Nothing to get excited about."

"We'll put it on the posters," said Sharon. "It'll be a sell out."

"Like *Songs of Praise*" said Tub. "My mum says it's a disgrace. People only go because they'll be on TV."

"Think of the ticket money," said Stick in George's ear.

But George could only think of the tights and the frilly blouse.

It wasn't until they were about to leave that George realized that something was missing — again.

"Where's the gnome?" he said to Kev.

"At the Sports Centre," said Kev. "We forgot it."

"Forgot it?" said George. "How could you forget it? You were standing there with it when I left."

"It was after that old woman arrived and everybody started shouting," said

117

Julia. "We thought we'd better slip out quietly."

"Without the gnome?" said George.

"I thought Tub had it," said Stick.

"I thought you had it," said Kev to Stick.

George stopped them before the argument degenerated into a brawl.

"Somebody will have to go back for it."

"Not tonight," said Julia. "I'm sick of that gnome. No wonder you hate it, Kev."

It was agreed that Kev and Stick would go back for it in the morning and George left it at that. It had been a busy day.

When he got home the old Hoover was tied up waiting in the hall for him to take to the jumble sale. Bits of grass and weed still showed poking out of various tubes. His mum had bought a carpet sweeper. That didn't make him feel any better either. If they had been able to afford a new Hoover she would have bought one, wouldn't she?

Chapter Thirteen

When they arrived at the school hall next day it looked like a war zone. The way things had been going, they shouldn't have been all that surprised. Mr Hughes, the janitor, was having every kind of fit at the mess of the place.

"Window smashed as well" he was saying. "I tell you — kids today, they ought to be locked up, the lot of them. And who knows what else they've done. I'll need to go and check the rest of the school now and me with the bowling club finals in half an hour. It's a disgrace, that's what it is, a disgrace. I want this place cleared up by the time I get back."

He went off still muttering and left them in peace to look at the devastation. Tables were overturned. Clothes, books, toys, furniture, everything lay jumbled on the floor.

George stood there with his mum's Hoover in his hands.

"It was all in nice neat piles when we left last night," wailed Julia.

"Who would want to break into a jumble sale?" said Tub.

"I suppose we're going to have to clear it up," said George. It looked worse than his bedroom on a bad day.

"I don't suppose that Hoover's working," Julia said.

George shook his head, "It's all jammed up with weeds. I don't think it'll ever work again."

"We've only got half an hour before the doors open," said Sharon.

"It's not fair," said Tub. "We didn't do it."

"No," said Sharon, "but we're responsible for the jumble sale so there's no use moaning. Come on," and she started to heave the nearest table upright. George looked at her in admiration and went to help. The others followed. Sharon smiled at George.

"I'll leave this to you, George," she said. "You're much stronger than I am. I'll just go and set up the table at the front door."

"Me Tarzan, you Jane," said Julia sourly as she disappeared.

It was nearly done by the time Kev and Stick arrived with the pram.

"Trust you to miss the work," said Julia.

"Any trouble getting the gnome out?" said George. Kev grunted. He was heaving the gnome into an upright position in the pram. It looked kind of weird.

"That doesn't look much like a gnome," said Tub.

"Horrible, isn't it?" Kev said with satisfaction.

Julia was looking puzzled.

"I've seen that before," she said.

"You saw it last night," said Stick.

"I didn't," said Julia. "It was all bundled up. I mean I've seen it somewhere else."

"Yuk," George said. "In a horror film maybe."

They all looked at the gnome. It had a sneering kind of wizened face and horns and, instead of feet, it had hooves. It was really horrible.

"Nobody is going to buy that, Kev," said Tub. "You're wasting your time. You'll have to take it home again."

"I can't take it home," said Kev. "My dad says he never wants to see it again and besides, somebody might buy it. There were two men round at the house last night when I was out asking if we had any garden statues for sale. Mum told them they had just missed this so maybe they'll come to the jumble sale and buy it."

Something flitted across the back of George's mind but Sharon came back in to announce she was just going to open the door and he let it go.

He pushed the pram behind a wardrobe. It was upsetting looking at that thing. Sharon took up her place at the door collecting the five pence entrance charge and they got started. It was quite a success. For one thing, everybody's mum came and bought something. George watched the growing pile of money with satisfaction. At least they would get the percentage this time. He had not forgotten the blouse.

Mr Martin looked in to see if everything was OK. The Headmaster turned up briefly and Sharon dealt with him. George sold a pair of roller boots to the junior called Amanda for seventy-five pence. They were old ones of his. Every so often the wheels locked and pitched you forward. He had stopped wearing them even before they got too small for him. He enjoyed selling them to Amanda. The only black spot was Stick's mum turning up with the dog and leaving it.

"Maybe we could sell it," said Tub.

Stick groaned and tied its lead to the pram. It jumped up and put its paws on the side of the pram and saw the gnome. Immediately it began to howl. Tub threw it a fizz bullet and it calmed down.

"Amazing how it likes those things," said Stick. "I wonder what's in them."

Tub looked at the one he was just going to eat and put it back in the paper bag.

They had been going for about an hour and a half and the money was mounting up nicely when it happened. Julia was wrapping up a stack of saucers for a customer when she gave a squeal.

"I knew I had seen it somewhere before," she said. "Look look, you lot."

She tore off a corner of the newspaper and thrust the half-wrapped saucers at the customer. The others looked at her in amazement. Her eyes were shining and she was almost dancing.

"Look," she said again, shoving the paper under their noses. "It's valuable. It says so here. There's even a reward. And you said this couldn't happen."

The rush had died down. The woman with the saucers left giving Julia a funny look. They were the only ones in the hall.

"What are you on about?" said George eyeing the money-box. Now was the moment. No customers. Sharon outside at the front door.

"Only that Kev's gnome isn't a gnome. It's the statue that's been missing from the museum for the last three months and it's valuable."

"Don't be daft."

"You're kidding."

"Not again, Julia."

"Kev, have you been pinching from the museum?"

Tub started to say something about the *Antiques Roadshow* and what his mum said — again.

They all looked at the paper. It was a bit crumpled and the photograph was smudgy but it was the gnome all right. There couldn't be two of them.

"I knew I'd seen it before. Remember the antique dealer pointed it out to us," Julia was saying when two men walked in.

Tub had started to say "hello" when the taller one reached across and snatched the paper out of Julia's hand.

"So the penny finally dropped, did it?" he said.

The thought that had flitted through George's mind came back and hit him like a hammer. Break-in at the school last night, two men at Kev's house asking about statues, two men at the Sports Centre locking them in the control room. It was the same two men.

"OK where is it?" said the tall one.

Nobody even tried saying "where's what?", not even Kev.

George leaped for the pram. Luckily there was a trestle table between him and the two men. He grabbed the handle of the pram and pushed.

"Catch," he yelled to Stick as the pram went hurtling across the floor. The dog, still tied to the handle, yelped as it tried to keep up. The gnome lurched and slid down amongst the blankets. Stick caught the pram. He also caught on to the idea.

"Catch," he yelled in turn to Tub as the men made for him and the pram went hurtling once more across the room. It was unlucky that in the game of pass-the-pram Kev was passing to Julia. Being small, she nearly got run over but the dog saved the day. As the smaller man leapt for the pram he tripped over the lead which was stretched out tight with the dog panting on the end. By this time those not involved in the passing of the pram had come up with the idea of getting on to the tables and throwing anything they could find at the enemy.

It was this scene that met the janitor's eye when he walked in. George thought he would burst. His face went purple and he could hardly speak. When he did his language was terrible. George thought of trying to explain to him but that was a nonstarter. The janitor wasn't the listening type at the best of times. Right now he was concentrating on being heard. The two men just happened to be on top of a table and the janitor advanced on them waving a broom and shouting about setting an example. They wouldn't get a better chance to make a break for it.

"Out," yelled George and they made a dive for the door.

The dog was a nuisance, tied to the pram. George scooped it up and threw it in beside the gnome. It howled and tried to get out but by this time they were building up a good speed and it shrank back and cowered in terror under the rug. Sharon rose as they passed, her mouth open.

"Hi, Sharon," said George. "Just taking the dog for a walk," and they hurtled past.

There was a crash behind them as the janitor and the two men burst into the corridor and bumped slap bang into Sharon. Her table fell over and George heard the sound of money scattering in all directions. He had a sudden, intensely painful vision of all that jumble sale money lying in the box in the hall — intact, untouched. Missed it again, he thought. The skateboard began to look doubtful.

They were half-way down the street before the two men broke free of the janitor and Sharon. George glanced quickly behind him. It wouldn't take them long to catch up, not out in the open. What they needed was cover.

"Into the park," he roared and steered the pram drunkenly through the gates. Delaying tactics — that's what they needed. Time to plan. Where in the park? The fountain, where they always went. No good, too open. Then again, maybe . . . A plan began to form in George's mind.

"Fountain," he gasped. He was getting out of breath.

Nobody argued. They wove their way in and out of pathways till they got there. They wouldn't be that easy to follow.

"Get the cherub, Kev," said George.

"What for?" said Kev.

"I've got this plan. Go on, Kev, you're the only one that's fit."

It was true. He wasn't even breathing hard. Kev went to get the cherub while the others stood around trying to get their breath. Julia was the first to recover.

"What's the plan then?"

"We swop the cherub for the gnome," said George, "then we let them see us, lead them away from the scene, dump the cherub and then come back for the gnome."

"Sounds daft," said Stick.

"Well, it isn't," said George. "You put something in a really obvious place right out in the open and nobody looks twice at it. We let them see us trying to hide the cherub, they think it's the gnome, right size, right kind of shape. We run away. They won't be interested in us. By the time they discover it's the cherub and not the gnome we'll be long gone. It's logical."

"And you've got the cheek to say I read too many comics?" said Tub.

"Will somebody give Kev a hand?" said Julia. "He's in plaster, remember?"

They were a bit wet by the time they got the cherub and the gnome switched over.

"It looks quite good up there," said Stick. "Lucky that cherub was loose."

"That wasn't luck. I've been throwing stones at it for years," said George.

"What about the dog?" Tub said.

It didn't look any happier sharing the pram with the cherub.

"Leave it where it is," said George. "It'll just get in the way otherwise."

The trick now was to get some distance from the fountain then let themselves be seen. They were creeping round the back of the tennis courts when there was a yell from the other side.

"We've been sussed," said Stick.

"Let's go then," said George.

"Where?"

"Out of the park for a start," said Julia.

They took the bottom road out over the common. As they passed the remains of the cub hut Tub suggested leaving it there.

George looked back. The enemy was in sight. He hesitated.

"No. Too open," he said. "They'd discover the switch too soon and be after us again."

He cast around for a hiding place. The common was depressingly open. Then down at the far end he caught sight of the old house.

"How about there, in the house?" he said. "We'll stash it in that cupboard where you found the vase then let them see us running away without it. It'll take them a while to find it and that'll give us time to go back for the gnome."

They pounded off across the common towards the house. The pram rocked and bounced. The dog kept its head down. Only the odd yelp told them it was still there.

It was the dog that was their undoing. Or, to be more exact, the undoing of the dog. With all the running and bouncing and suchlike, the knot on its lead had worked itself really tight.

"Cut it," said Tub hopping from foot to foot.

"What with?" said Stick.

"Unclip the lead," said George.

"I need the lead or the dog will run away," said Stick concentrating on the knot. "Wait a minute. I think I've got it."

"Wrong," said a voice from the door. "You've had it."

Chapter Fourteen

They stood in the doorway looking like the Incredible Hulk and the White Dwarf.

"OK" said the big one, "let's have no more nonsense and you won't get hurt."

Nonsense was the last thing on George's mind. He got the feeling the big guy meant what he said.

Tub tried to get into the cupboard out of the way as the two men bore down on them. The taller one wrenched the blanket off the pram and the dog yelped and bared its teeth. It was a puny effort but the man drew his hand back quickly. George made a mental note that he did not like dogs, even insignificant ones tied up to prams.

"That's not it, Joe," said the smaller one looking at the cherub.

"Shut up, Fred," said Joe. "I told you, no names."

No names, thought George. They weren't exactly Brains of Britain.

"Where's the statue then?" said Joe.

Nobody answered.

"Want me to persuade them?" said Fred.

Joe shook his head, "No rough stuff," he said.

George's spirits lifted.

"Not yet," Joe continued.

George's spirits fell.

"We're not telling you," said George. "You can do what you like to us but we won't tell."

It sounded good and he didn't think his voice had been shaking.

"What?" Tub squeaked.

"Oh, come on, George," said Stick. "I'm no hero even if you fancy yourself as one."

"He's right," said Julia coming unexpectedly to George's rescue. She turned to the men. "You're thieves," she said, "and thugs, threatening to beat up children."

George looked at her in amazement. It wasn't so much her standing up to them — just that nobody had called Julia a child for years and got away with it.

"And if anybody else talks," she went on, "they'll have me to deal with."

Even the dog cringed. With Julia in this mood nobody was going to argue.

"Who me?" said Stick.

"Never crossed my mind," said Tub sadly.

"How did you know we had it anyway?" said Kev to the men.

"You were seen," said Joe, "attacking it with a pickaxe. Do you realize how much it's worth?" He seemed quite upset.

"No," said Kev. "How much?"

"Look," said Fred, "we haven't got all day to stand here jawing. Let me duff them up."

Joe seemed to consider it this time.

"It wouldn't look good," said George, "beating up kids."

He could see Joe thinking about it, Fred too.

"Into the cupboard," said Fred.

They got into the cupboard. Fred pushed the pram in after them.

"We'll leave you to think it over," he said. "See how you feel in a few hours' time."

They heard the sound of a key turning in the lock.

"That guy's sick," said Tub. "He's got a mania for locking people in cupboards."

"Maybe it's just us," said George. "Maybe we bring it out in him."

There was silence for a moment then George spoke again.

"How come he had a key for this cupboard? I didn't see one in the lock before."

"This must be where they stash their stuff," said Kev.

"How d'you mean?" said George.

"Stands to reason," said Kev, "I mean this is where my dad found the gnome in the first place, only the cupboard wasn't locked. He thought it was just junk. Brought it home for Mum."

"They must have left it here till the heat died down," said Tub.

"Comics again?" said George.

"You should talk," said Tub. "Look where your idea got us."

"There was nothing wrong with my idea," said George. "I mean, if Kev had said this was where the gnome came from I wouldn't have suggested bringing it back here, would I? No wonder they got here so fast."

Tub had been lost in thought. "The guy that chased you with the pickaxe must have told them where you lived," he said now.

"He didn't have the pickaxe," said Kev, "I had the pickaxe."

"It doesn't matter who had the pickaxe," said Tub, "the point is, who was that guy that chased you?"

"I don't know," said Kev. "Just a guy with a hard hat and a clipboard."

"Must be from the council," said George. "They all go around with hard hats and clipboards. They must be going to demolish this place soon."

"And that's why those two came back for the gnome," said Stick. "When they heard it was going to be knocked down at last."

All this time Julia hadn't said a word. It must have been a strain on her for now she exploded at them.

"We should be trying to get out of here instead of standing around talking."

"How?" said Stick.

"George?" said Julia.

George shook his head, "Don't ask me."

"What's wrong with you?" Tub said to him. "Where are all the bright ideas?"

But George had no bright ideas — for once.

"Look around," he said. "The door's solid, the walls are thick, even the floor's in good condition. It must be the only bit of the house that isn't falling down and we have to be stuck in it. Why don't we just save our strength, wait till they come back and make a break for it."

"If they come back," said Stick.

"They'll come back," said George.

* * *

Two hours later he wasn't so sure, it was all very well saying they would leave them to think it over but this was ridiculous. He had visions of Fred and Joe being in an accident, lying in hospital somewhere, unconscious. Nobody would know they were here. They would never get out. In years to come there would just be a pile of bones and dust. Unless the house got knocked down round them. Then the bones would be dust as well.

Tub was moaning again about being hungry. They had eaten all the fizz bullets but five. They were saving those for an emergency. Funny how your idea of what was an emergency changed when you were locked in a cupboard, George thought. He leaned back against the wall and closed his eyes. Everything went black. It was several moments before he realized this was important. He opened his eyes again. Yes, he could see, dimly but it still wasn't completely dark. He closed his eyes again, just to be sure. Blackness.

"It's not completely dark in here," he said.

"If you're trying to cheer us up, don't bother," said Stick, "not if that's the best you can do."

"It should be completely dark," said George.

"Well, it isn't. Don't knock it," said Stick.

"There are no windows," said George.

"Look, George," said Tub, "we know you mean well but will you just shut up. It's bad enough being locked in here with the dog without you going raving mad as well."

"The dog's got claustrophobia," said Stick.

"I thought it was agoraphobia," said Tub.

"That was last week," said Stick.

George's eyes were turned up looking at the ceiling.

"The one place we didn't think of," he said.

Julia followed his eyes.

"Light," she yelled grabbing Kev. "Light."

"Light what?" said Kev. "I haven't got any matches."

"Light nothing, dope," she said. "Look, there's light coming through that hole in the ceiling."

"Not much," said Tub. His voice was casual but you could tell he was interested the way he was trying to climb up on Stick's shoulders.

"Get off," said Stick.

"You're the tallest," said Tub.

"Kev's the strongest," Stick said.

Everybody dived for Kev. He had never been so popular.

George got them sorted out. "Julia on Kev's shoulders. She's the lightest and smallest."

The ceiling was quite high but Julia could reach the hole. Her head disappeared.

"What's up there, Julia?"

"Another cupboard," said Julia. "The floor's rotten, just a few beams above this ceiling."

Stick groaned. "Just our luck, another cupboard."

"Not a locked one, idiot," said Julia. "The door's open. That's where the light is coming from."

"What are you waiting for then?" yelled Tub.

"The hole isn't big enough for me to get through," she said.

"You're the smallest. It'll have to be you," George said. "Try knocking away part of the ceiling. Even a little would be enough. You're so skinny."

"I'll get you for that, George Aitken," came Julia's voice.

Perhaps anger lent strength to her elbow or maybe she meant what she said. In any event, they heard her fist connect with the plaster and then the ceiling fell in. There was a yell from Julia and they looked up, eyes smarting, choking. As the dust began to settle they could see her legs dangling in the air.

"Kev," she yelled. "Where are you? This beam's going." True enough, the beam she was holding on to with what looked like her fingernails was beginning to sag and creak. Kev lumbered to his feet just in time. All at the same time it seemed his shoulders were under her feet the beam snapped and she was gone, scrambling up through the hole.

They all held their breath, waiting for the impact as she fell down again. Nothing happened.

"Julia?" said George.

Chapter Fifteen

"I'm OK," Julia's voice drifted down to them, slightly muffled. "I think I've swallowed some plaster."

"You shouldn't have had your mouth open," said Tub, picking bits of ceiling out of his hair.

"I was screaming at the time," said Julia. "It comes of being scared."

Her voice was stronger now.

"Hurry up and let us out," yelled George. "They could be back any time."

George's imagination had transferred Fred and Joe from their hospital beds to the front doorstep.

"I'm going," she yelled back, her voice receding. The rest looked at each other. They were covered in plaster dust. The dog shook itself and a fine film of dust rose in the air and started them coughing again. There was a rattling at the door and somebody kicked it.

"The key's not here," said Julia.

"They must have taken it with them," said Tub. "Isn't that typical?"

"How rotten can you get?" said Stick.

"Break it down," said Tub.

"Look, bonehead, if you can't break it down from your side I can't break it down from mine. George?"

"What?"

"What are we going to do?"

"I hate that question," said George.

He pondered.

"George?" yelled Julia.

"Shut up. He's thinking," yelled back Stick.

They stood there in respectful silence while George thought. He looked at the hole in the ceiling. There were still some beams that seemed to be intact up there. If only they had a rope of some kind. He dug his hands deep in his pockets. It was funny. In all the time he had spent in the cupboard it hadn't once occurred to him that he had missed the dress rehearsal with Sharon. It was the tights that reminded him. His eyes lit up.

"He's thought of something," Tub roared through the door to Julia.

"What?"

"Julia," said George. "Go up and see if you can find something, anything in that cupboard that will take Kev's weight."

"Why me?" said Kev suspiciously as they listened to Julia clattering back up the stairs.

"Because you're the heaviest," said George. Kev still looked suspicious.

Julia's head appeared above them. She started hammering on the beams. The beams started to crumble.

"Watch it," said Tub as a bit came crashing down on them.

"The beams are no good," said Julia.

"You don't say?" said Stick.

"Try to find something strong that you can tie a rope to," said George.

"I haven't got a rope," said Julia.

"No, but I have," said George. "Go on, Julia, get a move on."

"Where did you get a rope?" said Stick.

"It's not exactly a rope," said George pulling out the tights. His face was pale pink under the plaster.

Tub hooted, "You're going to let Julia know that? She'll have you for breakfast. She told you Sharon would make you wear tights."

"Do you have any better ideas?" said George.

Julia was yelling down at them again.

"There's the door handle. It seems OK."

"Right," said George. "Catch these and tie one end to the handle then let the rest back down to us." He threw the tights up and Julia caught them.

"Tights," she crowed. "I told you she'd make you wear them."

George looked at Tub, "One word, just one word."

Tub didn't say it.

A long black thing snaked down towards them.

"I've tied it as tight as I could," said Julia.

George looked at Kev, "You first," he said.

"Why me?" said Kev again.

"Because if it takes your weight it'll take anybody's," said George.

As it turned out, the tights were pretty strong. They weren't the flimsy variety. More what George's mum would have called "winter weight".

"It's like abseiling in reverse," said George to Kev. "You just grab the tights, put your feet on the wall and walk up."

"I've done abseiling," Kev said.

"I know," said George. "The Headmaster knows, the whole school knows about your abseiling."

The only real difficulty was getting started. Every time Kev tried to haul himself up the tights stretched even further until they could stretch no more. Once he was safely up the rest were confident enough to fight over whose turn it was. The only problem was the dog. George stuffed it down Stick's jacket and zipped it up tightly.

"Climb," he said.

Stick climbed.

At last they all sat on the top landing. George undid the tights from the door handle. The legs seemed to be about three metres long now but he couldn't help that. Losing the blouse was bad enough without losing the tights as well. For all he knew they might be family heirlooms too. Maybe they had belonged to her granny. There was a sound in the hall below them. They froze. George crept to the head of the stairs.

"It's them," he mouthed.

Nobody moved. He crept back to them.

"Look," he whispered, "the first thing they'll do is look in the cupboard. If we can get down the stairs while they're doing that we'll get clear away."

Nods all round.

They listened as the sound of feet crossed the hall.

"Ready to talk yet?" said a voice.

"Original, isn't he?" whispered Tub.

Still silence from the cupboard.

"Maybe something's happened to them," said Joe.

"Like what?" said Fred. "They're just playing games. Wait till I get my hands on them. Give me the key."

There was the sound of the key turning in the lock then a muffled yell.

"Look at this."

They would both be in the cupboard by now, thought George.

"OK," he whispered, "don't make a sound."

Stick stood up. There was a wriggling inside his jacket and the dog fell out with a thud. It immediately began barking.

"I always said you were too thin," said George to Stick as they threw themselves in a clump at the stairs. Kev took to the banisters. They heard the thud of feet as Fred and Joe came out of the cupboard like bullets out of a gun. The dog was leaping round their feet in a frenzy of excitement, barking itself silly. The lead wrapped itself round Stick's ankles and he fell in a welter of arms and legs. The others fell over him. The only one still in action was Kev. The banisters creaked ominously under his weight as he approached the bottom. Fred made a lunge for him. Kev's arm went out to steady himself and caught Fred just below the ear. It was Fred's bad luck that it was the arm in plaster. He went down like a stone, the banisters gave way and George, who had been wedged up against them, fell off the stairs into the hall below. He only had a moment to wonder if he was all right before Tub fell on top of him. By this time Joe was at the bottom of the stairs waiting, barring their exit. Fred had begun to groan so at least he wasn't dead but he wasn't showing any signs of wanting to get up either. George had a lot of sympathy for that. He felt exactly the same.

One by one they all began to struggle to their feet.

"Right," said Joe. "I've had enough of this rubbish. You talk and you talk now."

He stretched out a long arm and grabbed Julia.

"Unless you want her hurt," he said.

For the first time George began to feel really angry. Up until now he hadn't really taken Fred and Joe seriously — not deep down. But now — well, Julia looked scared and he hadn't ever seen her look scared before. She might be the world's biggest pest but she was only a kid.

Stick clambered down beside him, the dog close at his heels. "I wouldn't mind," he said, "but Mum would kill me." He had a funny way of showing it but he was worried too.

George looked at Julia. Her mouth was clamped shut to stop it from trembling. Joe's face grinned above her. Big lout, thought George, frightening a kid. Some tough guy he was, scared of dogs . . . That was it.

"Give me the rest of the fizz bullets," George hissed to Tub.

"They're for an emergency," said Tub.

George looked at him, "I'd hate to know what you would call an emergency. Hand them over."

"How can you eat sweets at a time like this?" whispered Stick as Tub handed them over.

"He's scared of dogs," said George softly.

"Stop mumbling and talk," said Joe.

Fred was beginning to move now. He rolled over on to his front.

"What if we set the dog on you?" said George keeping his eyes on Joe's. His hands opened the paper bag behind his back and the sweets dropped to the floor. The dog leapt on them.

"Don't make me laugh," said Joe. "That thing?"

"It might not be very big," said George, "but if you get bitten by a rabid dog you don't much care what size it is," and he moved back to reveal the dog.

It stood there grinning stupidly and from its mouth came bubbles of pink foam. There was even some dripping from its lower jaw. George knew it wouldn't fool him for long, not once he thought about it, but it might give them long enough. Out of the corner of his eye he could see the pram the men had wheeled out of the cupboard. Joe hesitated, his eyes fixed on the dog. His grip on Julia relaxed. George moved.

"Get Julia," he yelled as he lunged for the pram.

Fred was on all fours by this time. Kev launched himself in a beautiful rugby tackle at Joe. Stick grabbed Julia. Tub scooped up the dog and George was behind the pram. He pushed it with all he'd got. It glanced off Fred as it passed and he went down again with a thump. Straight as an arrow it made for Joe in the doorway. He dived aside just in time and the pram hurtled out on to the drive. George followed it.

"Run," he yelled.

They didn't need to be told. In fact they were running so hard they nearly ran into the mechanical digger that was rumbling up the driveway.

"Hey, you kids," said a man in a hard hat. "What are you doing in there? It's dangerous that building is."

And how, thought George.

"You going to demolish it?" he said as a van with 'Demolition Contractors' on the side drew up behind the digger. A couple of men got out.

"That's the idea," said one of them.

"Well, there are two men in there having a fight," said George.

"What?" said the other man. "We'll see about that. You kids get on out of it."

The driver of the digger climbed down. George looked back in time to see him lay a heavy hand on Joe's shoulder as he appeared in the doorway.

"That'll give us a bit of breathing space," he said. "Come on."

Julia was beginning to look a bit better.

"Thanks, George," she said as they trundled off across the common.

"Don't mention it," said George. "Your mum would have killed Stick if anything had happened to you. Anyway, it was Tub's idea really."

"What?" said Tub.

"That time when you said about frightening people with a rabid dog," said George. "I remembered it. Great idea, that."

Tub looked at him to see if he was taking the mickey. He didn't seem to be.

"I got it out of a comic," said Tub.

George grinned.

Chapter Sixteen

"Tell you one thing," said Tub. "I'll be glad to get home. I'm starving."

"We're not going home," said George.

"I am," said Tub. "I want my tea."

"You've missed it," said George. "Look at the time. If we hurry we'll just make the concert."

"You're not seriously thinking of going to the concert now," said Stick. "After what we've been through? Look at the state of us."

They were a sorry sight, bedraggled and covered in plaster dust but George was determined.

"If we don't make that concert we'll never hear the end of it. Now here's the plan."

They all groaned.

"I don't think I can stand the strain," said Tub.

"You're just scared of Sharon," said Julia. Gratitude didn't last long with her.

George ignored them. "We go through the park," he said, "swap the cherub and the gnome again and take it to the school. Then when the concert's over we explain everything to Mr Martin and get him to take it to the police."

"Why don't we just take it to the police now?" said Kev.

"Because we don't have time," said George. "Can you imagine how long it would take to explain and besides I can't think of anybody else that would listen to us. It might take a while to get him to believe us but at least he'll listen."

"My social worker would listen," said Kev.

"OK," said Tub, "so long as we go past the chip shop."

"First we've got to get the gnome back," said George.

It wasn't easy but they managed it. The cherub was listing slightly to one side by the time they had got it back. It looked drunk. They all got splashed with water which made the plaster congeal in horrible lumpy bits but nobody was much bothered.

They pooled their resources and managed three fish suppers and a couple of sausages for the dog between them. There was a bit of difficulty about getting served because of the way they looked. George explained that they were made up for a play they were doing at the school concert. The woman behind the counter smiled.

"Oh, yes, my Amanda's in that," she said. "I'm hoping to get along later myself. She's in the ballet scene but she hurt her knee roller skating. I hope she'll manage all right."

George smiled. The junior called Amanda and his roller boots. Life wasn't all bad.

* * *

They went in by the back door. The first person they saw was Mr Martin.

"Thank goodness you're here," he said. "Sharon's been jumping about like a cat on hot bricks."

Then he really looked at them.

"My God, where have you been? And what's the pram for?"

George opened his mouth to start to explain but Mr Martin waved him aside.

"Never mind. It's probably something I don't want to hear anyway. Now, are any of you in the choir?"

Stick owned up, "Sharon says I'm a baritone," he said.

"That's one of the nicer things she says about you," said Mr Martin. "Well, get on stage. The curtain is about to go up. And get cleaned up the rest of you."

Stick bounced off and Mr Martin disappeared to have a word with the pianist. The rest looked at each other.

"Mr Martin will listen to us," mimicked Julia.

"There's no justice in the world," said Tub.

"You go and get changed," said George. "I'll wait here with the gnome."

The other three were in the next item — a Red Indian ballet. Kev was playing the bongo drum. It had been pointed out to him that bongos weren't Red Indian but he wasn't easy to reason with. Julia was doing her rotten ballet and Tub was to be tied to a stake in the middle of the stage. He had seemed quite happy about it till they told him it wasn't that kind of steak. Luckily Sharon was also in the ballet, being a beautiful Red Indian maiden. She was supposed to rescue Tub. In fact Sharon was in everything. She had worked out this incredibly complicated costume change routine. It would have done justice to a professional, but it didn't leave her much time between scenes.

George hid behind the pram as the choir came off. He saw Sharon fly past to get her Red Indian maiden costume on then Stick came off. He looked as if he needed cheering up.

"Were you singing the same song as everybody else?" said George and Stick thumped him and looked better.

Julia, Tub and Kev arrived dressed for their parts. They had managed to get some of the plaster off but the general effect was a covering of pale mud.

"They'll think it's make-up," said George.

"Never mind that," said Julia. "You'll never guess who we've just seen out the back."

"The TV people," George groaned.

"No, they're out the front," said Julia. "It was Fred and Joe."

"How would they know we were here?" said George stunned.

"The concert got good publicity, remember?" said Julia. "What are we going to do?"

"I REALLY hate that question," said George. The Indians were beginning to take their places on stage.

"Take the gnome," said George.

"Where?" said Tub.

"On stage," said George. "Right out in the open."

Stick groaned, "Not again. It's the same plan, you know. Can't you think up anything new?"

"No," said George. "Can you?"

Silence all round.

153

"Just put it in the middle of the stage, Kev."

"That's where I'm supposed to be," said Tub.

"Well, you won't be. I'll need you," said George.

"But that means Sharon will have to rescue the gnome. She'll go mad," said Julia grinning.

"You don't dance in this thing do you, Tub?" said George.

"No, I just stand there," said Tub.

"No problem then," said George. "That's what statues are good at — standing there."

There were hisses from the stage.

"You'd better get going," said George as Sharon appeared.

She looked at George in horror. "What on earth have you been doing, George? You'd better get cleaned up and changed. We're on next, you know. And I hope you know your lines. Where were you this afternoon anyway?"

George muttered something but she wasn't really listening.

"Come along," she said to the others and she swept out on to the stage. Kev hefted the gnome and staggered after her closely followed by Julia, grinning broadly. There was just time to see the surprise on the Red

Indians' faces as Kev plonked the statue down in the middle of the stage then the music began and the curtain went up.

"Come on, Tub," said George.

"Where to?" said Tub.

"I want you to find Mr Martin. Tell him everything. I don't care if he doesn't have time to listen. Sit on him if you have to but tell him."

"What about me?" said Stick.

"You stay here. Make sure that gnome doesn't come off the stage for anything — anything mind."

"What are you going to do?" said Tub.

"Keep them away from the stage," said George.

He grabbed the pram. "Now get going."

One thing the council had done when they built the school — they had given it a really professional stage. There was some idea that it would be a community theatre. So it had all the bits, a curtain that went up and down, backdrops, flies, the lot. George made his way carefully towards the corridor at the back of the stage. He saw Fred and Joe almost at once and they saw him.

I'll have nightmares about this for years, he thought as he made off in the other direction. From the stage he could hear Kev pounding away on the bongo drum. He slewed round a corner and found what he was looking for, the stairs that led under the stage. If he could get them down there and lock them in they'd be safe. He left the door deliberately wide as he bumped the pram downstairs. They would have to come down after him. If he could hide till they'd gone down the far end he could get back up the stairs and jam something against the door.

It was dark below the stage. Above him, feet thudded rhythmically. He picked his way through the boxes, ropes and props that littered the floor. From the head of the stairs — nothing. Surely they must have seen the open door. The dancing above seemed to be coming to a crescendo. For the first time it occurred to George that he was on next. He couldn't honestly see any prospect of it and what was the point anyway? He had no costume, he was covered in plaster dust and stuck under the stage. He pulled out the tights. Best be prepared anyway, he thought. They were so long and thin by this time, he had a lot of difficulty getting them on. And even when he pulled them right up to his chest there was still about a metre flapping about at the end of his feet.

There was a burst of applause from above. It drowned out the sound of Fred and Joe coming down the stairs. It was only when Fred fell over something and swore that

George realized he had company. It wasn't surprising Fred had bumped into something. The floor was covered with stuff. George had found one of the few clear places. He scrambled to his feet as quickly as he could, cursing the dangling ends of the tights. It wasn't going to be easy running in them and he was going to miss his scene in any case. The applause had died down now. By this time Sharon would be half into her Juliet costume. All in all he was beginning to feel it was far better if he didn't appear anyway. There was more crashing about from the other end of the room.

"See if you can find a light switch, Fred," said Joe. "It's black as pitch down here."

"You sure he came down here?" said Fred.

"Where else could he have gone?" said Joe. "Just look for a switch, will you?"

George stood very still. In the dark it wasn't easy to place them and he didn't want to run straight into them. At least he knew the direction the stairs were in. When they found the light switch he'd make a dash for the stairs while the light was still blinding them. He heard a muffled voice from above announcing the next item then Fred's voice, "I've found a switch."

George tensed.

"Then don't just stand there," said Joe.

There was a sound of a switch being thrown and George felt the ground tremble beneath him. He thought briefly of earthquakes then, unbelievably, he felt the floor rise under him. He staggered slightly. There was a dazzling light above him as the stage seemed to open up.

As he ascended, blinking in the light, he heard yells from below him closely followed by a great burst of laughter. He looked at the audience in dismay and then at his feet as the trap door closed over the ends of the tights. Trap door right enough, he thought. He tried to move. No good. He was well and truly caught. The audience had begun to applaud. He turned away. The first thing he saw was the gnome, centre stage, grinning evilly at him. The next was Sharon. She was standing on a raised balcony thing and her expression was worse than the gnome's.

"What do you think you're doing?" she hissed.

"I'm stuck in the trap door," said George.

"Where's your costume? You look ridiculous."

"I'm wearing the tights," said George.

He looked down at his legs. She was right. He shouldn't really have put them on over his jeans. The applause had died down. The audience waited expectantly.

"Get on, then," hissed Sharon.

George's mouth went dry. He suddenly couldn't remember a word of his speech. Shakespeare, he thought. Sharon was tapping her foot impatiently.

George spoke, "I'll met by moonlight, proud Titania," he yelled. Then he dried up completely.

The audience roared.

"That's the wrong play," said Sharon. "Will you do it properly or get off."

George looked at his feet. Short of taking the tights off he was stuck. He couldn't remember a line of what he was supposed to say. He looked wildly at the sides of the stage. Surely somebody had the script. What he saw froze his blood. On one side Fred, on the other Joe, just waiting for the curtain to come down.

All at once George made up his mind. He turned to the audience and for the first time saw the TV cameras. That did it. Nothing in his entire life could be worse than this. He looked at the audience. The audience looked back at him — expectantly. He was thoroughly fed up.

"I'm fed up," he said to the sea of faces. "Just fed up. I've been locked in the Sports Centre, locked in a cupboard and now I'm caught in this trap door and all because of that gnome."

He pointed at the offending object. Incredibly, there was a smattering of laughter from the audience. He turned on them, furious.

"You may think it's funny," he yelled. The laughter spread. "But I don't," he went on. "I knew it would be like this. I knew nobody would believe a word of it." He could hear Sharon making squeaking noises behind him but he plunged on regardless. "Can't you just listen for a minute?" he roared at the audience. Some of them began to clap and George realized with a sickening feeling that they thought it was part of the show.

"This is real," he yelled, dancing about in his agitation.

The tights, held firm in the trap door, pulled him off balance and he fell to his knees. There was more applause and he looked up and found the eye of the TV camera staring at him from the back of the hall. He got slowly to his feet. The applause died. He tried to keep calm.

"Look," he said reasonably. "This is not part of the show." He pointed again at the gnome. "That," he said, "is the statue that was stolen from the museum. The one that's been in the papers . . ."

He waited a moment to let the audience get a good look at it. There was a flurry at the sides of the stage and out of the corner of his eye he saw Fred and Joe disappear.

"Surely some of you must recognize it. Somebody must have been to the museum. Its picture was in the paper," he said desperately.

There was a murmur among the audience as they craned to get a better look. At least they had stopped laughing. There was a crash and a thud and Fred and Joe reappeared running up the centre aisle, making straight for the TV camera.

"That's them," yelled George. "They're the ones that stole it."

There was another scatter of laughter and a few whoops from some of the audience. George groaned. Maybe it was a defect in his personality. Maybe he was doomed to go through life not being taken seriously. Well, it wasn't his fault. Nobody could say he hadn't tried.

Tears of frustration stood in his eyes so he couldn't see quite clearly who it was that jumped up suddenly out of a seat in the third row and began to shout. It looked like a demented dwarf.

"That's them. That's the kidnappers I told you about, Jenny. Get them, somebody."

Immediately there was pandemonium. People were out of their seats. Children were yelling. It was real audience participation.

The last thing George saw as the curtain came down was the Headmaster sitting in the front row with his head in his hands.

"I'll never forgive you for this, George Aitken," said a voice behind him.

George twisted round in time to see Sharon's face as she climbed over the balcony. It rocked slightly under her weight and gently folded up. George ripped the tights off and was running before she got to her feet.

Chapter Seventeen

The hall was very quiet. The audience had gone home. There was none of this rubbish about the show must go on. The show was wrecked and everybody knew it. The TV crew was happy enough. They went away saying things like — great television and — human drama, even though the police had impounded their film. They said it was evidence. Fred and Joe hadn't been caught but the inspector said not to worry. As far as he understood it was all on film and they would have no trouble identifying them. The curator of the museum had been called and, after thanking them, had personally seen to the crating of the gnome. He fussed over it till he got it out of the building and into the van that was to take it to the police station. It was evidence too.

Mr Martin and Jenny had explained to Jenny's aunt that there had never been a baby and had taken her off home.

"Hi, Kev," Jenny had said. "Turning into a solid citizen at last? I had a word with your mum earlier on and she says she's not having a patio after all. Something tells her it's not meant to be. She thinks your wild garden will be more restful." Kev had looked embarrassed.

"That's my social worker," he said to George.

Sharon had gone home after an interview with the TV people. She had a few pointed words to say to George about the return of the velvet waistcoat and the antique blouse.

"You can keep the tights," she said generously.

"Thanks a bundle," said George. He was going off Sharon Taylor.

Finally only the Headmaster was left. He looked at them sadly, "I don't quite know what to say," he said but he carried on anyway. "I'm in no doubt that you have all done very well in getting the museum's statue back. Indeed the curator was telling me it's the only really valuable piece the museum possesses. An early Corinthian figure of the Greek god Pan as I understand. However, I cannot help but feel that the cost has been considerable."

Too right, thought George. All that percentage money. He would never get the skateboard now.

The Headmaster's arm swept around the hall. Rows of seats were overturned and on the stage bits of scenery bulged through the curtain. From under a chair came a faint yelp and the dog slunk out.

"Nevertheless," the Head went on, "only a few people asked for their money back. Most seemed to enjoy the entertainment. In fact one or two said it was the best show they had seen in years. So, I think I shall have to let it go at that."

There was a roar from the entrance and Mr Hughes, the janitor, stood there.

"What's all this then? Turn my back on the place for five minutes and this happens. All I did was nip out for a quiet pint. Well? Who's going to clear it up then? That's what I want to know."

The Headmaster vanished so quickly George looked around for another trap door.

It was a full hour before they had the place tidied up to the janitor's satisfaction and he let them go.

"It's not fair," said Julia. "You'd think we would get more thanks than that."

"The guy from the museum was pretty pleased," said Tub.

"Do you think we'll get the reward?" said Stick.

George winced, "Reward? That would be a laugh with our luck. Do you realize we haven't made a penny on this? The concert takings were our last chance and we didn't get near them all night."

"Imagine that gnome being valuable," said Kev. "What's a Pan?"

"Oh, shut up, Kev," said the rest and the dog bit him on the ankle.

They were called into the Headmaster first thing on Monday morning. The Inspector was there. So was the curator of the museum. The Headmaster coughed.

"You'll be glad to know that the two men involved in the theft have been caught," he said.

"Once we had the TV film it was no bother," said the Inspector. "They've been in trouble before but nothing as big as this. I've just been telling your Headmaster we need more youngsters like you."

George could see the thought of more youngsters like Kev haunting Mr Redfeather.

The curator was speaking, "I understand you have also been raising money for school equipment. Very commendable, I must say. It's good to see children doing this sort of thing. There are too many people ready to condemn youngsters without . . ."

Julia couldn't stand the strain.

"Do we get the reward?" she said.

He looked at her as if he would like to condemn her.

"Of course," he said. "I have it here and I shall be very happy to divide it among you but first I must just say a few words . . ."

He went on for ages but finally he had to hand over the money. They stood there clutching the crisp notes. Tub remembered to say thank you and the rest chimed in as well. They could hardly wait to get out.

"I might get a drum kit," said Kev. "I really enjoyed those bongos."

Tub was wondering if you could buy a season ticket for the Wimpy.

"What are you going to spend yours on, George?" said Stick.

George stared at him.

"What do you think? The skateboard of course."

What a question.

"I'm going to get it lunch-time before somebody changes their mind about the reward."

But first he had to go and get Sharon's blouse back.

"Here's your eight pounds," he said to the man in the antique shop. "I'll have that blouse back."

The man picked it up and pointed to the ticket. Ten pounds it said.

"But it was only eight we owed you," said George, "for that thing we broke."

The man leaned across the counter.

"Look, son," he said, "Eve got a business to run. Overheads, rates, wear and tear. I can't sell at the price I buy. It's not business. Everybody's got to make their percentage."

George handed over a ten pound note. He couldn't argue with economics. After all it was what he had been preaching to the rest.

In the end he had to wait until after school to go for the skateboard. He could feel it under his feet as he raced to the shop. The swoop of it, the speed, the smooth running, wind rushing flight of it.

He was out of breath by the time he got there. For a minute he stood looking at it in the window. Then, unbelievably, as he looked at it, it turned into a Hoover. He rubbed his eyes and it was a skateboard again. I must be cracking up, he thought and he pushed open the door of the shop.

"I want to buy the Hoover in the window," he said to the shopkeeper and a horrible cold, slimy feeling came over him.

The woman looked at him as if he was mad.

"You're in the wrong shop, dear. Hoovers next door at the electrician's."

George couldn't believe it was happening. It was not like him. It just WAS NOT George Aitken. Even when he found himself next door at the electrical shop handing over all that lovely money for a second hand Hoover — a HOOVER — he still couldn't believe it. It was even worse when he got home.

"But, George, it was your reward money."

His mum was pleased. You could tell by the way she was talking to him — accusing him.

"What made you do it?"

"I don't know," said George miserably.

She smiled then. "Come on and get your tea," she said. "You can try the Hoover out on the weeds later."

What was worrying George more than anything was what he was going to tell the rest when he turned up without the skateboard. He couldn't tell them he had bought a Hoover. He couldn't think what had come over him. He broke out in a cold sweat picturing their faces. As for what Julia would say . . . He wondered if he was old enough to emigrate.

They made the evening news that night. The police had released the film. George saw Sharon being sweet about "the social responsibilities of young people today" then the film cut to Fred and Joe tearing up the aisle. He could see himself in the background with his mouth open and the tights stuck in the trap door.

His mum came into the room.

"How did you get on with that fund raising?" she said.

George scowled, "I'm finished with fund raising," he said. "I don't think I'm cut out for business."

"Fund raising isn't business, it's charity," she said.

George opened his mouth to say something uncharitable about charity but she was still talking.

"Did you get your parcel?" she said.

George looked up, surprised.

"What parcel?"

"I left it in your room. It came today but with the Hoover and all, I forgot all about it."

"I haven't been up there yet," said George.

He wondered who on earth could be sending him parcels. He never got parcels. Then, when he saw the long oblong box lying on his bedroom floor, he thought — Oh, hell's bells, they've sent me a plastic replica of the gnome for a memento.

But it wasn't. He ripped the paper off and there lay a box with a picture on it and inside the box, the real thing. It looked a million times better than Sharon Taylor. A letter fluttered out and he read it through quickly. He looked from it to the skateboard lying in its wrapping paper. He couldn't believe it. He'd won the competition — the mug's game. He had even forgotten he'd entered for it.

Bits of the letter jumped out at him "congratulations", "most original name", "most entries Star Wars type names", "makes a really eyecatching label".

He looked at the skateboard again. HIS skateboard. And he wouldn't have to tell the rest about the Hoover.

On one corner was a picture of a rearing horse with feathery things sticking out of its sides.

"Mum," he yelled. "I've won the competition. I've won the skateboard."

His mum came to the bottom of the stairs.

"What?"

"I've won. They're going to use my name for the skateboard."

She looked puzzled.

"What — George?"

171

He was hanging over the banisters.

"No, Pegasus."

"And who's Pegasus when he's at home?"

George's voice rang through the house.

"A mythical winged horse," he shouted. "We did it in Classical Background."

His mum's face broke into a smile.

"See what I've always told you about sticking in at school," she said.

But George was down and out of the door before she had finished speaking.

She watched him as he launched himself down the street on the skateboard. His voice floated back to her as he whizzed round the corner, arms outstretched on either side of him — like wings.

"PE — GA — SUS," he yelled as he flew.

About this author

This is Helen Magee's first children's book. It was written in tribute to her father who made her laugh with the stories he told her as a child, to authors who made her laugh as a young reader and to her children, now teenagers, who have always been able to make her laugh. She hopes the book will do the same for the children who read it. It is not a serious book.

Printed in the United Kingdom
by Lightning Source UK Ltd.
130757UK00001BA/45/P